A RAVE
COME

God's Faithfulness to Jessie and Wilfrid Stott

Wilfrid Stott

The Lutterworth Press

Cambridge

The Lutterworth Press
P.O.Box 60
Cambridge CB1 2NT

British Library Cataloguing in Publication Data
Stott, Wilfrid
    A raven will come: God's faithfulness to Jessie and Wilfrid
Stott
    I. Title
    266.0092

    ISBN 0-7188-2833-X

Cover illustration by Maggie Mason

Printed by The Guernsey Press Co. Ltd
Guernsey, Channel Islands

Contents

The Title

A RAVEN WILL COME - Why this title? As a family, whenever we were short of something, we got used to saying, "Oh, a raven will come"; in other words, God will provide as he provided for Elijah in the Bible by way of the Raven.

"So he went and did according to the word of the Lord ... And the ravens brought him bread and flesh in the morning and bread and flesh in the evening; and he drank of the brook."

I Kings 17, v.5,6

Preface

Called to China

What a great privilege to be called to the oldest surviving civilisation in the world; to the land which had the largest population of any country; to the land which until 1911 had been ruled by Emperors in splendid magnificence; to a land which for centuries had been under a civil service appointed solely on scholastic merit; to a land which had invented printing a millenium before Europe; and to a land which possessed the Great Wall and the Grand Canal.

Yet, this was a land which had thrown out the Imperial House and was in constant turmoil, as we discovered when we arrived there, a land disturbed by civil wars under ambitious war-lords, later to be invaded by Japan and then torn in two between the Kuomintang and the Communists.

It was into this turbulent period that we first came to China, then immensely proud of its glorious past, but quite uncertain about its future. Jessie had spent her first five years on the borders of Tibet in West China, and through meeting her father, I had become deeply interested in that country. What was it to mean in our lives?

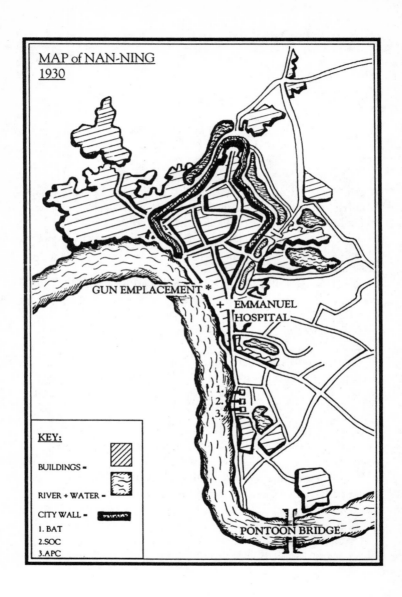

MAP of NAN-NING
1930

GUN EMPLACEMENT *
                    + EMMANUEL
                      HOSPITAL

1.
2.
3.

KEY:

BUILDINGS =

RIVER + WATER =

CITY WALL =

1. BAT
2. SOC
3. APC

PONTOON BRIDGE

1

Wilfrid's Story

"God is faithful, by whom you were called "
My father, the Reverend Percy Stott, came of an architect's family in Oldham, Lancashire. His father had designed a number of the Lancashire cotton mills. Three of his brothers were architects. However, my father became ordained and was curate in a well to do parish in Bolton, Lancashire. On the outskirts of Bolton was an estate, with a private chapel, owned by a Colonel Ainsworth. He had been converted in the Moody evangelistic campaigns and felt that he would like to influence the clergy in Bolton. He invited them up to a meal and a service in the chapel to hear William Haslam, the Cornish clergyman, preach. It was the first time, my father said, that he had ever heard the Gospel message, and he re-dedicated his life to God in a new way. When he had told his Vicar, the answer he got was that he could not stay in his parish, but must leave.

Colonel Ainsworth had the gift of several livings on that side of Bolton, and when St Peter's, Halliwell, became vacant in 1900, he offered it to my father who ministered there for the rest of his life, My mother, who came from a brewing family in Maidenhead, had also been converted, and between them they brought us up in a godly atmosphere.

I was the ninth in a family of eleven, ten of whom grew up. My father had a firm belief that the Word of God made it clear that it was the privilege of Christian parents to claim God's blessing on their children even before they were born and it was into this atmosphere that my life commenced. I was born on 12 August, 1904, during a mission in Bolton. I was considered the weakest of the brothers, and not strong enough to be baptised in church, so the baptism was performed at home. As I look back over the years I am sure that God called me to himself before I was born. I cannot remember a time in which I did not have a deep reverence for God. I am sure today that he was leading and teaching, and that the prayers of my parents, godparents, and a godly nurse, were from the earliest days being answered. It was not until I was about sixteen that I realized in fact that I belonged to Christ and began to enjoy the realization of this privilege. How I thank God for the careful Bible teaching of my mother, Sunday by Sunday, and the biblical teaching of my father. All the time, the Heavenly Father kept and restrained me from taking wrong paths. Surely 'God is Faithful.'

It was in a parochial mission, led by Mr Hudson Pope, that I first made a public profession of following Christ. Again, I am sure that it was God's hand leading. I was then at Manchester Grammar School. For two or more years I had been a boarder at Monkton Combe School in Bath but inflation following the First World War, had made it impossible for my father to keep my brother and me there. From Monkton Combe, with its strongly Christian emphasis, to Manchester Grammar School was a big change and I found the atmosphere at the latter, with the constant challenge of bad language and bad habits, much more demanding for a Christian, but the God who had called was faithful and enabled me, in spite of many failures, to maintain a pure and straight lifestyle. There were only too many lapses and failures in the Christian life, but at least I was kept from bad habits.

After the Mission in which I had made a profession of following Christ, I began to lose my first enthusiasm and grew cold. This was brought to an end in a curious way. It was the day of the congregational tea. I arrived a bit early and drifted into the room where the tea was being prepared. One of the helpers, Mrs Miriam Nuttall (the daughter of my godfather), later to have a big influence on my life, handed me a dish of butter and said, "Oh, do sit by the fire and melt this for us." I did so, and something more than the butter melted, and I found myself being drawn, through her, into active Christian service, a Sunday School class in the little mission church in Barrow Bridge, and helping in the large children's meetings on Sunday and Wednesday nights, of which she was in charge.

A little later, using Miriam Nuttall's large drawing room, I started, in fear and trepidation, a Boys' Crusader Class, at which she played the piano. God was beginning to lead and guide. Mrs Nuttall was led to start a girls' class. When I had to give up the class my two elder brothers, Oliver, who later ran the Southampton class, and Charlie, a doctor, became involved in the Lord's work.

My father had been one of those trying hard to stop liberal views on the scriptures penetrating the Church Missionary Society, of which he had been a lifelong supporter. He became one of the founders of the Bible Churchmen's Missionary Society (B.C.M.S.) to uphold the Biblical faith in the Church of England. Naturally, I had become deeply interested in its development and work. About this time the Reverend Walter Kitley, my future father-in-law, interested me in the needs of Tibet on China's western border. It was at this time too that I first met Jessie, then about 17 years old. I shook hands with her and I can recall only that she did not have a word to say to me then! Her father had been working for a number of years in that region. He was now Area Secretary for the B.C.M.S. So in my last year at school I offered to the B.C.M.S. The Honorary Secretary, the Reverend D.H.C Bartlett, was encouraging. They would like me to go to the University and to be ordained.

From a scholastic point of view, my life at school had been very perfunctory. I had no difficulty in being near the top of the form, but was far too keen on games to work well. I could have done much better and am amazed that the High Master, Mr J. L. Paton, encouraged me in the desire to become a missionary. So the call from the faithful God continued in spite of my slackness and unworthiness.

Mr Paton wanted me to go to Cambridge, but my father, owing to the fact that my eldest brother had been affected by liberal views at Cambridge, was against this. It was decided that I should do an external B.A. with London University, taking four subjects - Latin,

Greek, Economics and Chinese, and attend lectures at Manchester University, doing Greek and Latin on my own at home. When the results were announced, I had passed in Greek and Latin, but failed in Economics and Chinese.

I wrote to the B.C.M.S. saying that I would like to be sent out without further study, as the heathen were dying and I would rather not wait longer. It was, in fact, utter stupidity and I had no idea what the Lord had in store for me. They insisted that I should take it again, and instead of Chinese, I should take Hebrew. In fact, this was clearly the Lord's overruling for my taking Hebrew led me on to the teaching of Theology, in England, in China and in Kenya. How wonderfully God's faithfulness in His call is shown.

This time I passed and it was decided that I should go to St John's Hall, Highbury, and take the London B.D. If I could pass in one year (those with a B.A. were excused the intermediate exam) then it would be possible to be ordained in 1927 - there was no A.C.C.M. selection board in those days.

The only person who could have seen me through in one year was Professor Harold Smith, and he took this on: another of the Lord's generous provisions. When the results came out, I had passed.

The Society then wanted me to do a curacy in Bristol and to spend most of the week teaching in the recently formed B.C.M.S. Missionary and Theological College at Clifton as the first resident tutor. This again was splendid training for me in what was to lie ahead. All the students except one or two were bound for the Mission Field. So I had, as I mixed with them, splendid examples of devotion and zeal, especially in the Saturday night Open Air meetings at Bristol Bridge and in the prayer times of many of the students. I am sure that I learnt far more from them than they from me. There were light hearted incidents; for instance, a student pointed out to me that in the notes I had given them on the prophecies of Isaiah I had said that in the reign of Manasseh in 697 BC., tradition says that Isaiah was sawn asunder and that in the next section on the arrangement of the prophecies I had said "Isaiah naturally falls into two parts". Another amusing occasionw as when

I was correcting the answers of the only married student. When asked for the main events of Isaiah's life and the dates of his prophecies, the student had written 'In 720 BC. Isaiah married, and for some years he remained silent.'

In the spring term I had a bad attack of the prevalent 'flu and was sent home to convalesce and to see the heart specialist, Dr Brockbank, in Manchester. After his examination his verdict was, "You have a heart condition and must not think of going abroad. You must take no violent exercise and live a sedentary life." This seemed to rule out missionary service. So I went back to College in the summer term under these orders. Would God be faithful to the call He had given me?

In the summer term, I returned to the College. I felt I could not sit still. Perhaps unwisely, I began to play tennis and cricket; there did not seem to be any ill effects. I had agreed to go in the summer holidays as Chaplain to a boys' camp in North Wales. While there a climb up Snowdon was planned. I decided, again perhaps in a foolhardy spirit, to give my heart a real test. So I went up at full speed and got to the summit before anyone else. Again, there seemed to be no ill effects. Was God overruling the specialist's diagnosis?

After the summer vacation, I went back to the college. The Principal, Dr Sidney Carter, asked me if I could let him know whether I was going to China, as in that case he must look for someone to take my place. The Society had not asked for another medical examination. I decided to consult Colonel Middleton West, a missionary doctor and a keen Christian who had been in the Indian Medical Service and in Burma. What did he think I should do? His advice was to go to China and see how much I could do. So I told the Principal that, all being well, I intended to go to China. But I still felt that I wanted assurance from God that that was His will. I wrote to my father and explained it all. Before Christmas a verse that I had never noticed before, came up three times in my reading. 'Be of good cheer, for he shall strengthen thine heart.' It seemed to come as a special confirmation of God's will.

Dr Bartlett, the Honorary Secretary of the Society, asked me to spend the weekend with him at Wootton Bassett, where he was Vicar. On the Saturday evening he invited me into his study and asked me where I would like to go as a missionary. I replied, "To Tibet, through China, as Tibet has no missionary work." Then he asked me if I was willing to go anywhere that the Society wished to send me. After a moment's hesitation, I said "Yes, I think I am willing." Then came the shock. "We would like to send you to South China to build up the work that Dr Letchmere Clift and his wife have handed over to the Society."

I don't think that I made any reply, but it was all against my inclinations. Was not South China already well worked as a Mission Field? Were there not many missionaries already there? It was not the pioneer evangelism for which I had hoped. But little did I realize that this, in fact, was my Heavenly Father's call. Neither did I realize then, as I found out later, that in that province there were more who had never heard the Gospel in their own language than the whole population of Tibet.'God moves in a mysterious way, his wonders to perform.' However, the Lord quieted my disappointment and I prepared to go to South China.

Together with the promise of God's leading was another promise (2 Thess 33) 'The Lord is faithful who will streng then you and keep you from evil' and God had given me a measure of strength, in spite of the fact that, of my seven brothers I was always considered to be the weakest.

So, with no extra medical examinations asked for by the Society, the plans went forward and on November 29, 1929, I sailed for China on the S.S. *Mantua*, seen off by my father. In my cabin he committed me to the Lord for the work ahead. It was to be the last time I talked with him.

It was a five week voyage to Hong Kong. I was sharing a cabin with three young Scottish tin miners going to Malaya. As soon as we passed Cape Ushant, we met stormy weather and I spent two days on my bunk. Later, I found that after a few hours, the seasickness abated, and I was up and eating.

On that first Sunday, after passing into the Mediterranean, the Captain asked me to take the service. After it had ended, I asked him if there was anywhere on the ship where I could be quiet as I was sharing the cabin with three others. His reply was "Padre, you can have the use of my deck behind the bridge, whenever you like. I will have a deck chair put out for you." So for the rest of the voyage, the Lord provided a quiet spot where I could be private, read and pray.

At Colombo, I had a new passenger sitting opposite me at meals and we chatted together.

Christmas on board ship is unique. My Scottish cabin mates asked me to join them for Christmas dinner. I asked for two conditions, one that they would not expect me to take alcohol and secondly that they would not get tight. It was very kind of them to invite me and they willingly agreed.

In the evening I was leaning over the stern of the vessel, watching the phosphorescent sea in our wake. Presently my table companion came and leant over with me. It was a lovely night. He said to me "How long is this going on?"

I said, "What?"

He replied, "Don't you know who I am?"

I said, "No."

He then told me that he was my fellow missionary going to China from Persia. He was Dr Hugh Rice who was to share much with me and we got to know each other. He said that he wanted to see what I was like before letting me know who he was!

The evening we were due in Hong Kong, I was standing with the Captain on his deck. Presently, he said, "I don't like that!" I could see nothing, but he pointed out to me a dark line on the horizon. "That is fog," he said. That night our siren was sounding most of the time.

In the morning we sailed into Hong Kong harbour. Hong Kong is an island, dominated by the Peak, some 1,500 feet above sea-level. The harbour separates the island from the mainland, Kowloon. There were wharfs on either side of the harbour, which was teeming with Chinese junks with their square sails, and motor boats and steamers tied up in midstream. Ferries plied between Hong Kong and Kowloon every few minutes. We tied up on the Kowloon side. Chinese carriers with poles across their shoulders and loads at each end were to be seen everywhere. The shops on each side of the streets were decked with hanging boards with the name in Chinese characters. Rickshaws, pulled by men, were to be seen everywhere. The calls of sellers of food and sweetmeats sounded in all directions. It was all so new and fresh, and varied smells of freshly cooked oriental food were tantalising. Only a hundred yards or so from where we tied up was the railway station with trains running to Canton.

On arrival in Hong Kong we were met by the Bishop's chaplain and taken to the Bishop's House, one of the oldest houses in Hong Kong. Dr and Mrs Clift, who had hoped to meet us, had been held up and arrived a few days later. They were a delightful couple who had done a great work in Nanning under the title 'The Emmanuel Medical Mission'. Dr Clift's name, as I soon found out, was a talisman in that Province.

We spent several days there relaxing, reading, and preparing ourselves for the work ahead. Then it was time to leave the British Colony and set off for the Kwangsi Province in South West China to which the Lord had called me and where the fields were ripe for harvesting in His Name.

2

The Work To Which
We Were Called

The conditions in China in 1930

Jessie's father, a missionary in Tibet for seven years, had gone out in 1898, just before the Boxer rising, when many were martyred. In 1911 the Empire came to an end, and China was declared a Republic. The abortive attempt of Yuan Shih Kai to become Emperor had failed, and there followed a period of civil wars: the period of the war lords, ambitious generals with their armies fighting amongst themselves. After the failure of the Communist rising in Canton, South China was plagued by the rivalry between Canton and the Kwangsi clique in the next province. The Canton party were loosely linked to the recently formed Kuomintang Government in Nanking. The Kwangsi 'clique' was led by four leading figures who refused to join the Nationalist Government. These four ruled from Nanning and Kweilin in the north of the province.

The Kwangsi Province

In 1930 communications in this province were very primitive. There was only one stretch of motor road from French Indo-China (Vietnam) to Lungchow, about fifty miles distant. All travel was by river boat or on foot. The currency was in complete disarray: a twenty cent piece had a different value depending on which year it was issued.

It was a province of great natural beauty, being particularly famous for its 'Stone Mountains', limestone cliffs rising out of the flat plains and in the distance looking like cathedrals. A great band of this formation spread right across the province. In the south it was particularly striking with the '100,000 great mountains' and in the central area were the Yao Mountains with a local independent King of that tribe.

Nanning, the capital of the Kwangsi Province

Nanning, translated as 'Southern Tranquillity', was now the capital city of the Kwangsi Province, its population about 100,000. The fifty foot high city walls still stood firm, except in the south where parts had been demolished. Most of the old six foot wide narrow streets had been widened to enable them to take traffic.

Until 1904 the capital of the province had been Kweilin in the north, where the Emperor's summer palace had been. Kweilin's language was Mandarin, but in Nanning the language of the streets was Cantonese.

As the new capital was a Treaty Port, there was a section by the river, south of the city, reserved for foreign firms - in this case, two British and one American. It was after China's capitulation in the Opium War that she ceded land in the different ports on which Western nations could build offices and houses for the staff. The British Tobacco Company, the Standard Oil Company of New York and the Asiatic Petroleum Company (British) were the firms built on the river side. Further up the river and south of the south wall of the city was the hospital where we were to work.

The only approach to Nanning was by the river or on foot. A number of diesel driven motor launches, often towing and so travelling very slowly, were the normal form of transport in Nanning.

Missionary work in the Kwangsai Province

Dr and Mrs Letchmere Clift, who had commenced their medical work in Kweilin, had moved to Nanning and built the three-storey hospital outside the South Gates. The Clifts had run the hospital independently of a missionary society, but in 1924, on the formation of the B.C.M.S., they had handed it, and the orphanage for unwanted baby girls, to the Society in the hope that the work would be able to develop and grow.

The Christian and Missionary Alliance from the United States had been the leading missionary society in the province and had churches in most of the big towns, with headquarters at Wuchow in the east of the province. The Southern Baptists had a large hospital and church in the same town. The Church Missionary Society had a hospital in Kweilin.

In Nanning, apart from Dr Clift's Emmanuel Hospital, there was a Roman Catholic cathedral with a French Bishop, a Christian and Missionary Alliance Church and a Seventh Day Adventist Hospital. From an Anglican point of view our work came under the diocese of Hong Kong. As I was the first ordained man to arrive, it fell on me to take the lead in the church side of the work and I was made the Secretary of it. As far as the hospital itself was concerned, Dr Hugh Rice had been transferred from what was then Persia, to take the place of Dr Clift, who was retiring.

Though based in Nanning, the area within the Kwangsi Province to which I was allocated lay within a hundred miles of the south coast and bordered on the Vietnam frontier. It had the reputation for being against the central government and was the area in which the Tai Ping rebellion started which continued throughout 1850-1860. This rebellion all but toppled the Emperor in Peking. It was a primitive area, and one of the poorest. One of China's longest rivers, the West River, flows through it, and eventually reaches the sea near Canton City.

The climate of that part of China to which we went was very hot in the summer from mid-April to the end of September. Except when there was a thunderstorm, the temperature stood in the nineties, and the moisture level was very high. One kept coolest by sleeping on bedboards. When she first arrived there, Jessie found this very hard.

3

Beginning In China

It was now 1930, and Dr Rice and I were to proceed as usual up the West River, the third largest river in China. For the first hundred miles or so we travelled on the larger river steamers, under a British flag. These steamers went as far as Wuchow, some two hundred miles from Hong Kong.

Also a Treaty Port, Wuchow was a busy trading centre, built where the Cassia River from the north joined the West River. Here, the West River was around 500 to 600 yards wide, the bank lined with floating wharfs approached from the shore by planks. Numerous small river boats floated on each side, in which a family would live, often with chickens or a pig in bamboo baskets on the stern of the boat. The centre part was covered with a matting roof where the family lived. On the hill behind the town was the Sun Yat Sen buildings, the University of Wuchow.

We were invited to stay with the Asiatic Petroleum Company agent in Wuchow, but on arrival there found that the river further up towards Nanning was closed through a civil war between the Kwangsi war lords and the Canton war lord. We waited a week or so, but there was no sign of an ending to the blockade, so reluctantly we returned to Hong Kong. Fortunately, I left one large packing case at the American Petroleum Company. Rice left a double barrelled shot gun. Later on we were both to be thankful about this.

Back in Hong Kong we stayed for a few days with the Clifts in their bungalow on Cheung Chow (Missionary Island), some nine miles from Hong Kong. It was then decided that, accompanied by an English-speaking Chinese gentleman, we should take the French coastal steamer to Vietnam, to Haiphong, then take the railway up to the frontier and use the Chinese bus to Lungchow, the City of the Dragon. From there we would take the river steamer downstream to Nanning.

At the time of embarkation, the Chinese gentleman had not appeared and we weighed anchor without him. As things turned out, he evidently had guessed what would happen in Lungchow. In two days we reached Haiphong and were welcomed by Miss Ruth Field, the B.C.M.S. lady missionary there. Haiphong was a busy port some miles up the Red River. As our French steamer drew near the coast, we passed many of the three thousand rocky islands formed from limestone, similar to the stone mountains in our part of China. A year or two earlier a French passenger liner had anchored in the river mouth and, while a dance was in progress, had dragged its anchors without the watch noticing, and drifting down river, struck one of these islands and had sunk. Many people lost their lives.

Haiphong was a very smart French city with every modern convenience.

The Annamese population, both men and women, wore white trousers, the men with long black jackets to their knees and a wide, stiff black headband. Many had blackened their teeth with enamel. Most chewed betel-nut and spat the red juice out on the pavements. Rickshaws ran everywhere.

From Haiphong, we took the train to Hanoi and changed for the uphill rail journey to Langson on the frontier with China.

When we reached Langson, and informed the Sûreteé that we were to take the Chinese bus to Lungchow, they seemed a little surprised, but the next morning we took our seats in the bus and soon came to Nan Kuan, the great South Gate of China, on the frontier between Vietnam and China itself. It stands in a valley between two hills, a very imposing building about sixty feet high with a great archway, twenty feet high, and over this the Chinese characters state that it is indeed the southern entrance to China. On each side of the archway high walls extend up the hills. The archway leads into a square about fifty feet across, and further buildings behind contain a number of rooms where the Customs Offices were located, together with a frontier guard. We passed the Customs without any problems but I noticed that a Chinese soldier with a rifle who boarded the bus was wearing a red scarf around his neck.

We completed the fifty mile mountain road to Lungchow in a couple of hours. It was a motor road, built by the French and metalled. It lay across a plain, past a very wide parade ground, where in the days of the Empire, the frontier guards exercised, and then through a mountainous area on to the plain on which Lungchow was situated. The West River, already around one hundred yards wide, flowed through the town. We hired porters to carry our luggage across a steel bridge, built by the French. The Mission compound, where two lady missionaries looked after twenty Chinese orphan children, lay on the far side of the river, surrounded by high brick walls. It was to this house that we went on our arrival at the beginning of the week.

They seemed very surprised that we had come. "Didn't you know that Lungchow is in the hands of the Reds?" they asked. Dr Rice and I told them that we had no idea that this was so. We discussed the situation together. Miss Lucas, the senior lady missionary, was about fifty. Miss Loudwell was much younger, and had only been in China a year or two. It was decided that we should keep a low profile and not go outside the high walled compound. We also decided to hold a Communion service on the Wednesday two days later. This would be for the Chinese helpers as well as for the missionaries.

Meanwhile, we started language study with a Mr Li who was much later to become the Hospital Treasurer. On the Wednesday, about midday, he came to Miss Lucas and told her that the Communist leaders had shot the French Consul, the French Commissioner of Customs and the French priests and they were coming to shoot us the next day. What were we to do?

Neither Dr Rice nor I knew much Chinese, so escape would have been impossible, especially with the ladies. The only thing we could do was to stay put. We would carry on with the Communion Service as planned. So at about 7.00 pm, we gathered with our Chinese helpers to celebrate the Lord's death for us. It was a moving experience, taking the bread and the wine and not knowing whether this was to be our last day. We decided to spend the night, partly in prayer and partly in sleep.

Nothing happened until breakfast time. While we were eating, the gatekeeper burst in, white-faced. "They have come," he said. Rice and I went to the front door.

There were about fifteen Red soldiers covering us with their Mauser rifles, probably because we had our hands in our pockets and might have had revolvers. They had come, they said, to search the house. At first they were fairly well behaved, but on the arrival of an evil looking officer, they became much more careless. However, I experienced one friendly action. One of them gently took the wallet out of my breast pocket, opened it and held up some tens of French piastres, beckoned me into another room, put them back, and put the wallet back in my pocket. He put his fingers to his lips, as if to say "Keep it quiet," and left me. However, it was not long before they began to take things. I saw one man walking off with my old school blazer!

After an hour or so, Miss Lucas told us that we were to be marched to the Military Headquarters. She told us to pick up anything we could carry. She had wisely packed a little bag. All four of us as we were led out found that in one hand we had our Bibles (I have still got mine). In the other hand I had a pair of pink pyjamas!

Across the bridge we had passed over on our arrival we were led to the Military Headquarters. As we entered the yard, my eyes fell on a carpenter making a seven foot high wooden cross. Just for a moment the thought entered my mind that we were to be crucified, but he was only making a support for building an arch.

We were taken into the guard room and to our surprise found the French Consul and his metisse lady there. They were to be part of our party. He appeared to be very angry understandably enough. We sat there for more than an hour while a local soviet decided what to do with us. It was a trying wait, but at last we were led out and I saw a line of soldiers with rifles. 'The firing squad', I thought, but no, Miss Lucas told us that we were to be marched into Vietnam. The soldiers with rifles were the guard.

After a little while we set out with some soldiers in front, some behind. This was the road over which the bus had taken us when we arrived, so it was to be a march of around fifty miles. The weather was fine, but we knew it would be a very trying walk for the ladies. The first few miles were flat over the plain round Lungchow. Then we would enter the mountainous area where only a little while before brigands had held up a bus and made Miss Field, one of our missionaries, kneel at the side of the road while they robbed the passengers. Beyond this hilly area, the road passed through a market town and on to the frontier. The French Priests and the Commissioner of Customs had taken this road in their attempt to escape. Clearly it would take us much more than a day to cover it. How would the ladies cope? On the way, one of us picked up the page of a book. It was evidently dropped by the priests as they tried to escape.

A stall at the roadside was selling bananas and eggs. I felt very hungry, having only had half a breakfast. I bought some of both. The bananas were easy, but how to eat the eggs? Finally I decided that the only way was to crack them on my teeth and swallow them raw. Fortunately, they proved to be fresh.

As we began the ascent among the hills we suddenly found ourselves under fire from the hill opposite. It was a brigand band. Afterwards, we learned that they were holding the French priests, and the Commissioner of Customs. At the time, the four of us missionaries were lagging behind. Evidently the brigands thought that if they could wound one of us they would get a higher ransom. I ran on; Hugh Rice waited to help Miss Lucas who was finding the going difficult. Some of the soldiers were deployed and came behind us, but we were soon out of range, and no one hurt.

The ladies found the going more and more difficult. As we walked, Dr Rice and I, of course, could not talk to our guards but it was thrilling to see Miss Lucas explaining the Gospel to these Communist soldiers as they crowded round her, in spite of her tiredness and exhaustion.

At last, after twenty-five miles, we came in sight of a derelict farmstead, and the word went round that we were to stay the night there. Hugh and I were put into one room with the doors taken down on which to sleep. The ladies were in the next room. Opposite, I could see the dim light of an opium lamp as the officer smoked. There were no mosquito nets and no bedding, and we spent a far from restful night, in our clothes, with nothing further to eat. We could just hear the ladies discussing all the things that they had lost. At least we could thank our Heavenly Father that so far He had kept us safe, and we committed ourselves into His hands.

The next morning we were up at dawn and were on the road without anything to eat, marching another seven miles in the stillness of early morning, seeing the smoke rising from little homesteads here and there. Finally we reached P'ang Cheung, a market town, and were led to a Chinese restaurant. Here, because the French Consul was known to the people, we were all given a most welcome Chinese meal, steaming hot and appetizing, to which we did full justice. To our surprise on coming out we found we were to be taken in pony traps, two in each, with the driver and a soldier armed with a Mauser.

So the cavalcade proceeded until we met a French car which had been sent to pick up the French Consul and his metisse lady, so that they would not have to walk any further. In trying to turn on the narrow road it had been backed over the edge and stood on its rear end some seven feet below the level of the road in a rice field. The soldiers gathered a group of local men and it was soon on the road and away with the French Consul.

Meanwhile, we continued to the great South Gate of China and alighted to wait for transport across the frontier. The telephone kept ringing and the thought kept coming to us that perhaps they had changed their minds, and we were to be taken back. At last a Chinese bus arrived and we were very quickly outside the area of Red influence. How grateful we were that the Lord had brought us safely out, having lost only our possessions.

In Lang Son the Resident's wife, who spoke some English, insisted on taking us round the shops to purchase essentials. Rice and I had two days' growth of beard and had to begin to get cleaned up. He was wearing an old sports jacket, out at the elbows. We spent the night in the Hotel de France. Next morning, we caught the train for Hanoi and Haiphong. Sitting in the train, I realized what a help it had been not to be alone, but to have had fellow missionaries with me, in contrast to Christ who went through his sufferings alone.

Miss Lucas and Miss Landwell did not come on the train. In fact, a few days later Miss Lucas heard that the Red Army had withdrawn a little way from Lungchow so she went back, risking her life, and brought the orphans and Chinese helpers out to safety. If ever an action deserved the Victoria Cross, it was that.

Why these Communists treated us so leniently, we never discovered.At about the same time John and Betty Stam were beheaded; others were shot. Messrs Besshardt and Hayman, all of the China Inland Mission, were held to ransom. The two Communist leaders of our encounter were brothers, Yu Tsok Paak and Yu Tsok Yu, both, if I am correct were Kwangsi men and had probably heard of, if not experienced, Emmanuel Hospital's care. Perhaps that was the reason. It was certainly God's intervention for our preservation. How deeply we were grateful when we reached Haiphong, for the Annamese chauffeur, a Christian, who invited us to go out for a Chinese feast. He said, "Now that you have nothing, I may invite you out!"

The Society were not very pleased that Dr Clift had allowed us to go to Lungchow by ourselves. He was hardly to blame for he had planned that we should have a Chinese guide.

Before long we went back to Wuchow, this time to stay at the Christian and Missionary Alliance Headquarters on the hilltop across the river. Here we commenced language study in earnest and at the same time had the opportunity of getting to know their missionaries who had been the pioneers in missionary work in that Province and also the missionaries of the Southern Baptist Hospital.

From early March until the end of June, 1930, we waited, not very patiently, for the river to open up again, so that we could proceed. Had we been experienced missionaries, we could easily have walked the distance in a week. But perhaps it was a good thing we did not for we were able to get to know the missionaries and especially the leaders of the Christian and Missionary Alliance work. Later it helped greatly in coming to an agreement not to overlap our areas of evangelistic outreach.

It also enabled us to get to know the Chinese leaders in the Christian and Missionary Alliance and perhaps to avoid a pitfall into which that mission fell, and which could have been avoided. I am referring to their policy of only allowing Chinese control where Chinese contributions made it self supporting. This, we felt was a commercial attitude to introduce into church relationships. Nor in fact, were their missionaries accepted as members of the Chinese church, as we Anglicans were.

At last news came through that a river steamer could get through because of a lull in the fighting, and was leaving, so, well advised by our hosts about provisions and water for the journey of a week to ten days, we embarked in a 'bluebottle' river launch. These steamers were so named because they operated with a continuous buzz.

In due course we arrived in Nanning. We had been impressed by some of the scenery we had been through and the perilous manoeuvring through the 'Rapid of the Suppressed Wave' where there had been so many accidents and where a temple had been erected to propitiate the spirits and secure a safe passage.

Emmanuel Hospital just outside the South Gate of Nanning was the tallest building in the city. The Hospital compound lay between two streets, one the main thoroughfare to the river bank. The church building was situated facing this road. Further in was the dispensary block, and behind that, the main hospital building with three storeys, and above that, the 'crow's nest'. This was to be my bedroom until my first furlough. It had windows on all four sides and so caught any breeze there was. The two lower floors were wards and above them the missionaries' accommodation. Outpatients were seen in the dispensary block. In the garden was a well with a Chinese-style tiled roof above and seats around it.

At this stage I was continuing my language studies, and some evangelistic work. It was now getting really hot. The temperature was not much above ninety degrees, but very humid, and it meant continual perspiration. Unless you used blotting paper under your hand, a letter was wet before you reached the bottom of the page. Mosquito nets were essential. There was no air conditioning and no refrigeration, so there was no keeping food for more than a day or so.

The really hot season is from late April until the end of September. Every three or four weeks, the temperature rises until there is a heavy thunderstorm then the temperature drops quickly, up to fifteen degrees or so. As the Province to the north is a plateau, some three or four thousand feet above sea level, when the wind comes from the north the temperature may drop some thirty degrees in an hour or two. At Nanning further south, the temperature rarely went below forty degrees at any time of the year. The West River is here some two hundred yards across, and in the summer may rise ninety feet. Towards the South the high walls around Nanning had been broken down, though the North Gate still remained.

We had not been there long when rumours began to circulate that a large army from Yunnan to the west, who supported the Nanking Government, was approaching to take Nanning from the Kwangsi clique. It was not long before, as we looked from the upper storeys of the Hospital, we could see lights on the opposite bank, and one day we saw soldiers. Those inside the city had built up the gaps in the city wall with brick walls and destroyed all the nearer houses outside the wall.

On 11 July, the A.P.C. agent, Humphreys, informed us that he had been told to leave in the Company's launch, the *Nanning*. He offered to take the ladies with him and on the 13 July they left Nanning for Hong Kong.

By 22 July the first shots were fired into the city from the opposite bank of the river and firing at night began on the 23 July. So Rice, Fryer and myself moved down from the Hospital building into the dispensary in case of stray bullets. The mosquitoes were very bad. On the next day we sent letters to the leading generals in both armies and hung out Red Cross flags.

On the 29th, at 10.30 pm, there was a sharp exchange of fire between the two armies. We saw that a four inch gun had been mounted on the city wall near the river; many refugees began to come into the Hospital grounds.

From 3 or 4 August, there was a lull in the fighting and the Yunnanese army had moved away from the town. Long ladders were sent up to the city wall. Rice and Fryer decided to join those climbing the ladders and see conditions inside the city. I was too fearful to go with them, but they managed to get back safely. With air raids occurring frequently and the desultory rifle fire, the Hospital was busy treating patients, sometimes for most of the day.

On the 8th there was an air raid attack from Canton on the South of the city where the brick wall had been erected and that night we saw Yunnanese soldiers outside the hospital getting ready for an attack on the South wall. Rice, Fryer and I were under the dispensary, the floor of which was three or four feet above the ground. Everything was deathly still until about 2.00 am when machine gun fire was let loose on the wall, replied to by a fusillade of machine gun and rifle fire from inside the wall. There was much shouting as the Yunnan soldiers charged down the street. Meanwhile the gun on the city wall opened fire and one shell hit the Hospital building and another landed in the garden. We were still underneath the dispensary. After some two hours it was clear that the attack had failed and the Yunnanese were withdrawing from their front line.

After some two days it was clear that there was to be another attack. This was preceded by a heavy air attack on the South wall, lasting about half an hour. Following discussion with the Hospital Staff, we decided it was wise to move away and occupy the three foreign residences on the Bend a quarter of a mile away and set up the Hospital in an old temple nearby. Fryer started in the evening with those who could walk. I went with the stretcher cases a little later, while Rice went over with the medical supplies. Rice and Fryer took possession of the Asiatic Petroleum Company house, while I occupied the British and American Tobacco Company house, with the Socony house in between.

On 12 August, my birthday, there was another abortive attack on the South Gate wall by the Yunnanese, and another shell hit the hospital.

Meanwhile, in the makeshift quarters, we continued treating patients and casualties and getting better sleep away from the firing line. The houses we had occupied were built on piles with a six foot high space underneath. In all three houses these spaces were sheltering dozens of refugees.

On the night of 25 August, I had gone to bed as usual, but at about 1.00 am I noticed a commotion among the refugees under the house. I got in touch with one of the Chinese nurses. She told me that in the Standard Oil Company of New York house next door brigands were searching, trying to find the Chinese agent who had the keys of the safe. As all was quiet, I decided to find out if Rice and Fryer knew.

I walked out into the Bund, the name given to that whole length of river bank, never realizing that if they had left a sentry I could easily be seen in my white pyjamas. I slid down the river bank and crawled round and came up opposite the A.P.C. Home. All was quiet. I called out their names, but there was no answer, so I decided they were still asleep. In fact, they were hiding among the banana trees in the garden. I went back as I had come and got into the B.A.T. house. All was still quiet next door, so I decided to go and fetch the police from their station behind the hospital.

I went behind the houses on the Bund as I felt I might be seen from the city wall. Halfway across the playing field, in the pitch dark, I saw the glow of a lighted cigarette end. One of the customs officials who spoke a little English told me that the brigands were not armed with guns and there were only a few. So I went on.

The Police Station had been evacuated, so I went into the Hospital to look for Rice's double barrelled shotgun. I thought perhaps I could scare the brigands. Fortunately, I could not find it. So, with the three hospital wardmen with bamboos, we went back to the B.A.T. house making as much noise as possible. When we got into the house everything was still quiet. They said the brigands had gone. When I looked over the wall, everything was still and quiet. I should have realized that, if the brigands had gone there would have been a great deal of noise. So after a while I went to bed and got to sleep. In fact, the brigands did not leave until 4.00 am.

The next day we discussed the situation. Law and order seemed to be breaking down. We decided that we should escape before we were held to ransom, as seemed likely, and so we made preparations to leave Nanning. Rice and Fryer had been in touch with the A.P.C. agent and got permission from the Yunnanese General to leave on the A.P.C. launch, the *Nanning*. The permission was only given on condition that the three oil company launches would tow barges on which some four hundred wounded Yunnanese soldiers could be taken to Wing Shun, some thirty miles down the river. The night before, these wounded were loaded on to the tow boats. We felt we must do all we could for them so the three of us with bandages, swabs, syringes and probes set to work about 7.00 pm, by the light of storm lanterns and continued till nearly 1.00 am, treating all we could. Most of the wounds were suppurating, and the stench was pungent; however, we eventually finished and snatched some sleep. The only medical training I had had was a St John's Ambulance course!

On reaching the launches on the next day, we found them occupied by the Head of the Customs, their families and masses of luggage. After a conference with the Yunnanese General we left on the Sunday.

There was a lovely view that evening. In front of us was the wide expanse of the river in the fading sunset glow. On the far bank were clumps of bamboo reflected in the still water. It was a delightful Sunday evening. The three of us sat on the front deck singing hymns.

Approaching Wing Shun at about 5.30 pm, we were just preparing to draw alongside the jetty when a shot rang out. Fryer and I made for the cabin and lay on the floor; Rice went into the engine room. For half an hour the firing continued. The launches and tows got out of control and almost rammed each other. One bullet ricocheted off a metal strut and nearly hit us. Eventually the firing stopped and we discovered that we had been mistaken for enemy troops coming down the river. No one had been injured and apart from many bullet holes, no damage had been done. How grateful we were to our Heavenly Father for taking care of us in this incident and so many times during the previous two months.

We learned afterwards, that the other houses on the Bund, the B.A.T., the A.P.C., Customs and Post Office had all been ransacked the night after we had left them. Chinese refugees, many quite well-to-do members of the community, were held to ransom, almost certainly by the same brigand gang. Again God's good hand had protected us.

It was not until April the following year that all hostilities ended and we were able to get back. Meanwhile, after some weeks in Hong Kong, mostly on Cheung Chow, the Missionary Island, and sorting out Mission accounts from Nanning, I went to Haiphong and was there until nearly 1931, doing language study and helping a little in speaking to the orphan girls, and in the evangelistic services.

It was during this time in Haiphong, when I was living alone in the church building and not feeling very well, that a great wave of doubt assaulted me. The thought came, "How dare you claim that all these 400 million people are wrong and you are right?" I said to myself, "Well this is the Christian belief."

"And how do you know that what the Bible says is true?"

"Well, our Lord put his seal on it."

"And how do you know that he was true?"

"Well, the sign he gave to prove his claim was the resurrection, 'Destroy this temple' and the sign of the prophet Jonah." So the test then was the genuineness of the resurrection and I began to go carefully into the evidences for the resurrection and came out with a much stronger faith in the truth of God's word and in the conviction that I was right in coming to seek to lead the Chinese to the truth. I was grateful to the Lord for confirming my faith in Him.

The New Year of 1931 brought about a cessation of hostilities, and the prospect of return to Nanning. The journey to Wuchow was not difficult, and at last Dr Rice and I secured passages on the 'bluebottle' called the *Wa Shang*, to Nanning.

However, it seemed as if the devil was determined to prevent our return. After some twelve hours progress from Wuchow, the steersman suddenly pulled into the bank. At first they said that it would proceed the next day. In fact, the main shaft had broken and had to be taken out. So here we were tied up at the side of the river with no houses in sight. Day after day passed. We were told that Chinese meals would be provided free, but we were getting very impatient.

It was a fortnight before we could proceed, but at last we reached Nanning and had a warm welcome from the Chinese staff. Things were now quiet and the usual hospital routine was continuing. Peace had been made with Nanking because the Kwangsi faction had come to terms with the central government.

Soon after this I decided to try to train two or three possible candidates as evangelists in a Short Term Bible School. We rented a house and they slept there and I went in to eat meals with them. I wanted to try and see if I could manage on the same food that they were eating. This consisted of two meals a day of rice and some vegetables, and sometimes a bit of meat. I tried this out for a month, hoping that I could live as the poorer Chinese did. At the end of the month my fellow missionaries insisted that I should give it up as I was getting thinner and thinner. So reluctantly I abandoned the experiment.

From my earliest days on the mission field, I felt sure that the highest priority should be given to developing Chinese leadership in the Church and this was the objective in the Bible School. Most of my time was taken up being Secretary for the work in South China. This involved a good deal of correspondence with the Bishop of Hong Kong and with the Chairman of the Christian and Missionary Alliance. I also helped with services in the Church especially because there was no other ordained man to take the Communion Services. A good deal of time was spent in preparing candidates for baptism and in evangelistic efforts. On occasions I went to Haiphong to take services there.

About the beginning of June 1931 we had a real test of faith. On the Saturday, Rice had asked me to go and knock a golf ball about on the disused aerodrome. The next morning as I got up I heard groans from Rice's bedroom. I went in and found him on the floor writhing in pain. He knew he had an acute attack of appendicitis. He asked me to get an aeroplane to fly him to Hong Kong. Of course, this was impossible; however, I did manage to get a taxi and driver to take us the first sixty miles over a rough unmetalled road.

It was a painful journey and every bump gave him acute pain. At the end of the journey we managed to get on a 'Noah's Ark', as we called them, a large wooden vessel high in the stern, towed by a steam launch, and so reached Wuchow, the halfway stage. There was a large Mission Hospital there, run by the Southern Baptist Mission and he could have been operated on there, but he was feeling better and insisted on taking the river steamer to Hong Kong.

We had not been going very long before he began to hiccough. He and I knew that that meant the appendix had burst and he had peritonitis. Unless operated on within 36 hours, it would be fatal.

We were due to spend some four or five hours at a place on the way down. When we got there I decided that I would see the Chinese Harbourmaster and ask if the vessel could be released more quickly, which would save a few hours. To this he agreed.

We reached Hong Kong in rather more than 24 hours and immediately I rang the Hospital on the Peak, 'The Matilda'. All the ambulances were out, so we had to wait another three quarters of an hour until one came. On arrival at the hospital, Rice was violently sick and as white as a sheet. We found that the surgeon was out and would not be back until 6.00 pm, very near the end of the 36 hours; however, in God's goodness, he operated in time and was successful. How thankful we were that the Lord had spared his life, and that the journey had been successful, overruled, as we were sure, by the Lord's good hand.

I returned to the Nanning Hospital by river. On arriving back at the Hospital, the question arose: should we close the hospital until the doctor was well enough to come back? There was an excellent Chinese nursing staff, though no missionary nurse. I asked them what they thought and it was decided that I should see what patients came and we would do what we could for them. So I used to see a patient in one room and go into the next room where there was a dictionary of treatment. It was a dangerous thing to do, but the Lord overruled and at least we were able to relieve quite a lot of suffering.

During these days I was trying to get a real grip on the language and decided that as one talked to either Christians or outsiders, they inevitably made sentences simpler than if they were talking to each other, so I would use a different method. In the hospital grounds there was a well with seats round it and the Chinese staff would gather there after dark, in the cool of the evenings and chatter together. I felt that if I could slip down unnoticed and sit there without being seen, I could listen to them talking to each other and learn idiomatic Cantonese. This worked very well. I began to grasp the way they would talk to each other. I am sure it was an idea from the Lord, Himself. Later I was to find that the more intellectual Chinese had a style much more difficult and often interspersed with allusions to the classics.

It was about this time that I began to notice the difficulty the country folk had in understanding when the preaching was in Chinese, as their tribal language which the Chinese called 'earth language', was completely different. It was only later that I discovered the real facts, and was led by the Lord to concentrate on reaching them in their own language.

One of the problems which I had to sort out as the Secretary of the South China Field (which I had been since I first arrived in China) and as the first clergyman sent to Nanning, was the problem of our relationship to the Diocese of Hong Kong in which we found ourselves. The name of the churches in the Diocese, both in Hong Kong and in China itself was 'Chung Hua Shing Kung Huei' (the Holy Catholic Church of China, hereafter C.H.S.K.H.). Dr Clift's name for the Nanning work which he had initiated was quite different. When I arrived, the Bishop was Bishop Duppuy, but by 1932 he had retired and been succeeded by Bishop R.O. Hall.

The B.C.M.S. had passed a resolution that there was to be "no Diocesanization". That, in fact, meant that they would not agree to a bishop making decisions about the missionary work of the Society.

Here perhaps I must explain that the authority of a Bishop in the Mission Field was very different from that of a Bishop in England. In the Mission Field the Bishop would make all decisions about where clergy should be located, when they could move and where, who should be accepted for ordination and to which Theological College they should go for training. He also made decisions about disposal of funds from England. Obviously, if the Bishop was liberal or modernistic, it would go against the very objectives for which B.C.M.S. had been founded.

So it fell to me to try to explain this to Bishop Hall and try to find a *modus vivendi* in which the Bishop could act as a father in God and we could give him the respect and honour due to a Bishop in England, and yet not have to accept his administration of the work. Fortunately, we both accepted this position and it was agreed that as the work expanded we would look forward to a time when the B.C.M.S South China Field could become a Missionary District and finally a new Diocese in the C.H.S.K.H., the Anglican Church in China. So we accepted the title C.H.S.K.H., and with this in view, we began to prepare to train our own clergy. I was truly grateful to Bishop Hall for his magnanimity in this. In the end, I attended the last General Synod of C.H.S.K.H. in Shanghai in 1947 as representative of the embryo Missionary District.

Another problem to be solved at that time was our relationship with the Christian and Missionary Alliance, the American Mission which had been doing the largest part of the evangelistic work in the Province. We were firm in our aim to come to an amicable arrangement to avoid overlapping as B.C.M.S. was determined to expand their work. After several talks with Mr Oldfield, their chairman, we came to a mutual agreement and divided the areas in which they and we would work. This worked well as time went on. Theologically, of course, we saw alike.

As I look back over those first three or four years when all of us missionaries were very young and quite inexperienced, I am amazed that we did not make many more mistakes. It must have been in answer to the many prayers that had gone up in the homeland and on the field. We could so easily have been involved in all kinds of blunders in our dealings with the Chinese, with the Diocese and with other missions. The Lord overruled our immaturity.

Another problem and one in which we came to an amicable solution was the method of evangelizing. Most missionary work in those days, not only in China, but in most mission fields, involved sending a paid evangelist, if not a missionary himself, to an unevangelized town or city, and for him to build up a congregation as there was a response to the Gospel. Gradually as they were able to contribute, the worker would be paid by the gifts of the congregation and the church would become self-supporting.

As the work developed, I began to realize, as I prayed over it, that this was going to limit the evangelization in two ways; the number of evangelists available and the amount of the Society's money available to support the evangelist. I had read Roland Allen's books 'Missionary Methods' and 'The Spontaneous Expansion of the Church', and began to wonder if something less dependent on Mission Funds was possible. In the end the plan adopted for the Southern area of our field was along the following lines.

Two 'hardy evangelists', with little more than an experience of conversion and a short term Bible School course, were sent to some unreached market town. Paid for by Mission Funds, they would stay either in an inn or rent a house. In those days people from all over the area congregated in the towns for the markets held every third day. If, after some months, there was no response, the evangelists were to move elsewhere as that place had had an opportunity of hearing the gospel. If there were people interested, then they were to stay on, concentrating on helping them, as well as evangelizing, meanwhile making it clear to them that they would be leaving at the end of two years. They were to watch and see who showed any signs of leadership. By the time they were due to leave, the one with signs of leadership was publicly set aside in a service of commissioning and the paid workers moved on. It was hoped that these incipient leaders would come in each year for a short term Bible School. The embryo congregation would either meet in a Christian's house, or would club together and rent a simple building. In one case they built a church.

This method had its weaknesses, but it seemed to work as well as, if not better than, the old method and enabled many more centres to be reached. The Bishop of Hong Kong approved and promised that in time when they had been tested, he would ordain these voluntary leaders.

It was into this situation in Nanning that Jessie arrived in February 1933, having spent years dedicating and preparing herself for God's service, in China particularly.

4

Jessie's Story

Jessie's father, the Reverend Walter Kitley, came from a market gardening family in Bath. He offered to the Church Missionary Society to go out as a missionary in response to the Horsburgh call for pioneers in West China. After training at the C.M.S training school in Islington, he sailed for China in 1898, just before the Boxer movement, which had been inspired by the old Empress Dowager. With the Reverend W.H. Aldis, he was wrecked on the rapids in the Yangtsze river, but escaped unhurt. It was not until 1903 that it was considered safe for his finacée, Lily Marks, to be sent out. They were married in 1903 in Ch'ungking in Chinese clothes and set up home in Mao Chow towards the borders of Tibet. Here he did evangelistic work, hoping to reach the Tibetans. During their furlough in 1905, Jessie was born at Combe Down, and when a few months old went back with them to the centre where they had been before.

Not long after, while travelling by river, the boat was wrecked. Mrs Kitley could not swim, and Mr Kitley had to decide whether he should swim ashore with Mrs Kitley, or the baby. Asking Mrs Kitley to keep hold on the wrecked wooden boat, he swam ashore with the baby and returned to rescue his wife and bring her to shore safely. Had it not been for that, this story could not be told.

Mr Kitley continued to seek to reach the Tibetan tribes across the border and became blood brother to one chief.

When Mrs Kitley contracted a goitre, they had to return to England in 1910, bringing to an end their missionary career. So Jessie had spent her first five years on the Tibetan border.

After a curacy, Mr Kitley became Vicar of North Newton, near Bridgewater. Later he accepted the living of Pennycross, a suburb of Plymouth. Here Jessie joined the Guides during the first world war, later becoming a Lieutenant. On one occasion she was practising semaphore on the cliffs and awakened the suspicion that she was signalling to some German ships at sea!

From 1914 to 1953 she kept a journal. It commences as follows. 'Through the wonderful grace of God, I took Jesus as my own personal saviour in Christ Church, Weston-super-Mare, in a talk to children, the speaker took as his subject:

S - Saviour
A - Almighty
V - Victorious
I - Infinite
O - Omnipotent
U - Universal
R - Received or Rejected

Thank God that through His mercy I could not bear to put "rejected" so I took Him at His word.' Though she loved the Lord from her earliest years, it was at this time in 1914 at the age of nine that she deliberately committed herself to Christ.

A chance remark of a girl friend, suggesting that she would follow her father's example and become a missionary, set her mind thinking and on 11 October 1922, aged 17, she wrote 'Praise His Name! I made full surrender in public at the "Keswick in Plymouth" last meeting, and heard the call of God to the Mission Field.' She wrote out the hymn, 'When I survey the Wondrous Cross', but changed the last verse to:

> Were the whole realm of nature mine
> That were an offering far too small
> Love so amazing, so divine
> *Has now* my soul, my life, my all.

'His, till He comes, consecrated to His service. The time since that full surrender has been the happiest of my life.'

'December 20, 1922 - First communion. Oh, what a precious time, a living communion with Him. How unworthy I am, and yet how loving He is, and what strength He gives.'

In March, 1924, she wrote 'Oh, how I ought to long to go out and tell those poor people of China about my Saviour. Surely he has not preserved us through all those five years in China unless He wants us for His service in that dear land. If He tarries, may He take me there.'

In April, she wrote, quoting a talk she had heard, 'It had to be won [the crown] off our own bat. Think of the great amphitheatre; God and His holy angels, the world, Satan and his angels. O God, grant that I may win this crown and win his "bravo, well done".'

On 1 June, she wrote: 'The winter seems to have impressed on me the sense of his approaching advent. Oh, if this year, this month, this week, this day, this hour, this minute should usher in His coming. Should I be ready and watching? Should I be ashamed of Him? What inspiring questions. Oh, may my Father prepare me more fully to be His and keep ever joyous the thought of His return.'

11 October 1924, 'The second anniversary of my call. Oh, what a blessed day this has been. Two years ago today I surrendered myself to Him in *public* and while singing that beautiful hymn 'When I survey the wondrous Cross' I heard the call of Christ to China. He has been very near and dear to me since then and I felt His presence while singing it this morning.'

The journal continues with the constant theme of thankfulness for God's blessings and short bursts of prayer that she may be kept faithful to Him and His call. On 15 March 1925, she writes 'Once again His holy day has come. May I long for deeper communion with Him of which I had some taste at Communion and before the evening service. Oh, *how* He loves.'

She celebrated joyfully the third anniversary of her call to the mission field that year. In January of 1926 she went for an interview to do nursing at The Royal Infirmary in Liverpool and was accepted for training to begin on 31 March of the same year. On her first day, her diary records her joy at having started the course.

31 March, 'My first day in hospital and the beginning of a new life for me. It is so wonderful to think that I have really taken this big step towards China - if it is the Lord's will - as I believe it is.'

In the first few months of her training she met Nora, a friend who became very dear to her. She prayed earnestly for her conversion and took her to the B.C.M.S. meetings in the hope that she would give herself to God.

She enjoyed the training, though it was difficult at times. She records in her diary how as part of her midwifery course later, which she did with Nora, she had to go to the notoriously rough Scotland Road area of Liverpool and had to be escorted there by another nurse for safety.

On the fourth anniversary of her call to the mission field, she re-dedicated herself to her Lord and on 31 October wrote 'I am willing now to lay myself in His hands if He sees fit to send me into the unevangelized lands of China. If this is His will for me, I am ready to hear His call - ready with this grace to face all the loneliness and discouragement and danger.'

On 7 July 1929, she writes 'Today I have definitely offered to B.C.M.S. for work in China. How blessed it is to know that I am not on my own: I am bought with a price.'

On 11 October 1929, she writes, quoting the famous hymn: '"I heard the call, come follow, that was all. Earth's joys grow dim, my soul went after Him. I rose and followed, that was all. Will you not follow when you hear His call." How these words express my deepest hidden feelings. O my Saviour, even though sometimes the light grows dim and the world seems so obscure, "I love, I love my Master, I will not go out free." Another, the seventh anniversary of my call has come. How wonderfully He has led me in the paths of joy and peace ... may I hide continually in the Secret of Thy Presence during the coming year. Whatever it may bring! Lord of my live, I once more come to thee and lay my life at thy feet.'

On 3 November she writes, 'Once more, my birthday, and I am 24. Another year of service is before me. I have renewed my vow to the Lord regarding China and have answered, "Here am I, send me."

O my God, if it is somewhere else instead of China, send out someone in my place for me who is ready to go now.'

After completing the nursing course, Jessie's decision to do the midwifery course proved a wonderful opening in the years to come.

In April 1931, she entered the B.C.M.S. Women's College at Bolton House in Bristol.

On 3 November she writes, 'Another year begun. What may it bring forth? He holds the key of the unknown and I am glad. This time next year shall I be journeying towards that needy land, or will "The King have come for His own?"'

Her conviction that she should be sent to China grew stronger:

4 May 1932, 'The Lord seems to be leading me through difficulty and misty ways during these days. At present China seems far off, hope and longing almost impossible of reaching. He has some loving purpose and plan awaiting me, of this I am sure and in *His* time He will reveal it. The deep heart longing and consciousness of His call still remains, but maybe He is going to use me in some other sphere, but this I know, the place of *His* choice is the place of the rarest blessedness, that can never be experienced anywhere else!!'

In the same month Miss Nellie Sandles, who was to be allocated to the mission field at the same time, said that the letters from the Society arrived for her and Jessie simultaneously and as they opened them, they discovered where they were to be sent. Jessie's said that it was to be Burma.

For years she had felt sure that it was China and she felt mystified. What had happened to bring this about? Why, when she had offered for China, was she being sent to Burma?

Unwittingly, I was responsible for her disappointment. I had been in South China for some three years and was Field Secretary. We had been thinking of the needs of the South China field. Only two centres offered accommodation for missionaries: Nanning and Wu Ming (Mo Meng). There were no married missionaries (the Bishop of Hong Kong laughingly called us 'B.C.M.S., the Boys and Curls Missionary Society'), and we felt it would be unwise to have any more unmarried lady recruits. There were five of them working

41

there at the time. I had written to the Society and asked that no more single lady missionaries be allocated to South China; so they had reallocated Jessie to Burma.

It was a very real trial to her faith. She wrote in her diary at this time, 'May every member of the allocation committee be conscious of an overpowering sense of God's presence and of *deep* responsibility.' Later in our life together, we discussed this and were able to laugh about it.

On 9 May only five days later, she wrote, 'The Lord has chosen Burma for my field of labour. I cannot tell how he is leading, but I am happy to know that he will lead along the path of His will. No one but He knows the *cost* of giving up the desire and longing of ten years, but praise His name, His peace now floods my heart and I can go *wherever* He leads the way.'

On the 11th she writes, 'Another test of my faith. I am staying another term at college. I will not say through a mistake, but in the wonderful leading of God ... there are no mistakes with our Master. So now as the Lord leads, I shall be sailing for Burma in the early part of 1933.'

In June, she writes, 'The Lord is marvellously burning Burma on my heart and unless he leads differently, I have "set my face" towards that land with *joy*.'

On 24 June she writes, 'What can I write? Words are superfluous. Blessed be the Lord God who only doeth *wondrous* things. Last night Miss Nevin told me that I have been reallocated to China and this morning I received the official letter ... I praise Him for the testing time for I have learnt many precious lessons ... I can *never* doubt my call to China because He worked so wondrously.' It is not clear exactly why the reallocation took place. It is possible that her father who was on the B.C.M.S. Committee influenced the re-thinking, knowing how sure Jessie was that she should be in China. In fact, she could not know that the Lord would in time send us both to Burma.

11 October, she writes 'The valedictory at Bath (the Mayor was present). How wonderfully God upheld and undertook and I pray

that some may have heard the call today, even as I did ten years ago. My heart is full of praise and thanksgiving for His graciousness and leading during the past years.'

Again, there seems to have been some doubt as to her being sent to China. She writes 'October 14th, 1926. This has been again a time of great testing; the Lord alone knows the greatness of the cost and the strain to feel that all is not settled. I felt during these days that the Devil was trying his utmost to close the door, and will do so; and so I have just laid hold afresh upon the promises of God and His almighty power that His will alone may be done, and now comes the time of joy, for once again the door stands open wide for "prayer was made unto God for me." Praise to His name, and as I face the great future, planned by His hand, I am conscious of utter unworthiness and of so much that needs His hands and touch upon my life. But He has called and He *will* prepare. Oh, that daily I may rest at His feet and learn of Him.'

14 November, 'He knows all it costs to give up home and loved ones and go alone to earth's darkest places to lay down life itself, it may be, in seeking souls for whom the Saviour died.'

5 January 1933, she writes joyfully, all doubts behind her, 'Tonight brings me to the eve of sailing for the land of China, His choice for me; and, through all the sadness, I can praise Him for all the way He has led me during my seven years of training. Oh, as I look forward to the time, short or long, in which it will be my *honour* to serve Him, I know He is in all the future. May I continually know what it is to be filled with His blessed spirit and empowered. My darling Mummy and Daddy experience the joy of His strength during these days. And now I close this diary and with it an era in my life. I praise Him for all His dealings with me of which this is a record and I look forward to a new experience of the wonder of His grace and power to *"usward".*'

So, on 6 January, she, Nora Bromley and Marjorie Bennett sailed from Tilbury on the *S.S. Corfu*, enjoying Christian company on the vessel and at some ports on the way. It was not until 22 February that she finally reached Nanning.

After what had seemed so many times to be impossible - reaching China, the land to which she knew she was called - she had, through God's good hand, arrived.

5

How The Lord Drew Jessie And Me Together

It was not long after arriving in Nanning on 23 February, that Jessie felt the Lord was drawing her in love to me. She gave no sign or hint of this. The plan was for her to be allocated to Wu Ming to do medical work there and to learn Mandarin. She was greatly relieved when she heard this, because it gave her a breathing space. She was to go there with another lady missionary.

Wu Ming (in Cantonese - Mo Ming) was a busy market town about 30 miles north of Nanning. It had been the home town of the former governor of the Province and there was a somewhat primitive road from Nanning on which there was a service of equally primitive buses, service being suspended if there was rain. The former governor had laid out a park in which there was a lake fed by underground springs. A branch of the West River flowed near the town beside which was a seven-storeyed pagoda. By the lake, a Chinese style summer house stood. The language spoken on the streets was, for the most part, the tribal language, now called Zhuang, but there was also some Mandarin spoken.

When she returned to Nanning, I had absolutely no idea that Jessie was becoming fond of me. She was immersed in language study which she took very seriously and she was also doing some midwifery work. It was not until the beginning of July that I began to feel drawn to her. I prayed that I would not make any mistakes. About the middle of July both of us began to realise that we were being drawn to each other.

In China it was not done to allow any outward signs of affection, so any approaches had to be quite unobserved. In my diary for 15 July, I wrote 'the first step taken,' referring, I think, to the first signs she gave me of being fond of me, while we were playing scrabble.

So, on 18 July, when she was studying in an empty first class ward of the hospital, I proposed and, as she put it in her diary, she was quite sure it was God's will for her to say "Yes."

Until the Society gave permission, it was not possible for us to be engaged; in fact, not until September. In a letter she wrote to me after I had proposed and been accepted, Jessie confided in me that after her friend Nora had become engaged, she had been moved to pray about herself. She told the Lord that she was quite willing to remain single if that was His will, but if His will was for her to have a partner, that He would be preparing her and her future partner for all that lay ahead, that they might be ready for God's will, whatever it was. She had continued for a number of years to pray this.

What a wonderful thing it was that after years of prayer on her side and a willingness to follow God's leading, and prayer on my part, we were drawn together. Her letters before we were married, while we waited for my return from early leave, were filled with the wonder of a new love and joy.

In writing to one another and in the times we were together we shared quite a number of the questions which would arise in our married life together. Both of us had an implicit confidence in the full inspiration of the Word of God and both of us wanted it to be our guide through our lives together, and this we began to share immediately.

Then, too, both of us had a firm belief in our need to be guided in our prayer life. Jessie had already experienced the answers to prayer in her allocation and in God's leading in regard to a life partner. I, too, had experienced the results of prayer and trust in ignoring my heart condition and being guided to South China, and in the preservation of my life in dangerous situations. So we shared this realization of the importance of prayer in our lives. We also shared a deep desire to get as near to the Chinese as we could. We wanted our home to be one to which the Chinese would not be afraid to come and feel at home, and that in dress we would get as near as was wise in those days. For this reason, too, we both wanted to get a good grip of the language and, if possible, to be fluent.

Then, too, we both wanted to commit to the Lord's hands the whole question of a family; if He gave us little ones, to trust Him to give us the needed grace as parents, and if He did, we committed the number of children to Him. We were sure that their coming would not interfere with the work to which He had called us. Later, we made it our habit never to have intercourse without first asking God's blessing on our union, treating it as a sacrament.

We were both sure that the Lord would provide for our needs. We would treat what money we had, not as our own, but as a trust from God, and would use it only as He guided. We had both been brought up to regard the Lord's Day as sacred to Him, not to be spent as we liked, but as a sacred time, in which to honour Him. I do not remember ever having to discuss it together; it seemed to come naturally. One agreement we made was that if we had a quarrel of any sort, we would not go to sleep without making it up, and apologising to one another.

Jessie had been brought up in her early years to realize that missionary work in China would mean facing many difficult and sometimes dangerous situations, but with God's grace we were ready. After our engagement, while I was in England on an early furlough of six months, Jessie went out many times with one of the evangelistic bands from Nanning. They would start in the morning and often walk ten to fifteen miles to reach some village. She had written to me before we were married about the evangelistic work: 'You know, darling, it is the longing of my heart to go out amongst the people. I would heaps rather be in a difficult place where we were really reaching the people than to settle down always in Nanning and not be able to do so much, and yet I'm content if it is His will. But, darling, my heart aches for these country women who don't get the opportunity of teaching. I long to be able to speak more so that I could really help them. Darling, you can be assured that I'm willing and full of joy to share the Lord's life of evangelism, if this is His plan for us. I'm fully prepared for such a life, if the way opens.'

Much later, when, on the eve of the Communist takeover in 1949, we were faced with the question of whether to return to Wu Ming and face what would come under Communist rule, there was no hesitation on Jessie's part, or mine, in spite of having to be separated from the family, the eldest two for four years, the next two for two years. We were sure of God's leading.

For five months Jessie concentrated on Mandarin, the language her father had spoken when she was a little child. After our engagement, she turned to Cantonese. These two types of Chinese with the same characters are as different as English and French. Cantonese has nine tones instead of Mandarin's five. After studying Cantonese for only six weeks, she gave her first talk at prayers on the Hilltop at Wu Chow on her birthday, 3 November.

As we were drawn together, I tried to express our thoughts in verse - 'The Two One' and then our hopes for our home in the poem, 'Home.' Looking back, I am sure that in spite of many, many mistakes, and failures, God was overruling and guiding us in the long years together, our union having been founded and built upon prayer.

Home

Thou shalt be host, dear Lord, in this new home.
To make it what thou wilt, dear Saviour, come
Our hearts' desire with thee here to abide,
To learn of thee, to lean upon thy side.
And day by day as thou dost break the bread
May we in joy commune with thee, the Head.
And as we work and as we rest to know
That daily we into thine image grow.

6

The Wedding

The bride in her wedding dress was standing at the side of the busy Nathan Road in Kowloon, Hong Kong. It was only 10.15 am, but it was extremely hot. In her white silk wedding dress, she had just come down the thirty odd steps from the Basel Mission Home on the hill behind, to wait for the car that was to take her to St Andrew's Church for the wedding. The car had already taken the bridesmaid, Grace James, and the Matron of Honour. Meanwhile she waited at the side of the road - ten minutes, twenty minutes, thirty minutes - and still no car. An interested crowd of Chinese gathered round. At last, after thirty-seven minutes, the car arrived. The Chinese driver had decided to have his rice after delivering the bridesmaid, before fetching the bride.

Meanwhile we had all been sitting in the church waiting, including the Bishop of Hong Kong.

As I stepped out into the aisle to meet her, she was just as lovely and unperturbed as ever, and quite collected. How thankful I was that nothing worse had happened.

After the wedding, she took her bouquet up to the Matilda Hospital, where the one who was to have been Matron of Honour was ill. It was just like her to be thinking of others on her wedding day.

We went for lunch to the Repulse Bay Hotel and in the evening caught the ferry from Hong Kong to Cheung Chow, an island about nine miles away, to begin our honeymoon in the New Zealand Mission bungalow. After supper, in the cool of the evening, we sat on the verandah looking towards Hong Kong island, with its twinkling lights. Everything was very peaceful and quiet.

But it was not to be so quiet as it started. A day or two later, after breakfast, I walked across a section of concrete about ten foot square outside the back door, to pick some flowers. It was very hot and all I had on was shorts, a shirt and gym shoes. Suddenly I heard a hiss behind me and looking around I saw, about three feet away, a five foot long cobra just swaying to strike. I had cornered it without knowing. The nearest doctor was nine sea miles away. Had it struck before hissing, the only thing that could have saved my life would have been for Jessie to have cut my leg off. It had hissed, and I bolted through the kitchen door. It was the narrowest of escapes.

Another time, as I moved a paper from a rattan table, there lay a small poisonous snake. During the honeymoon we experienced three typhoons which meant screwing down all windows and seeing that nothing was loose, at night as well as in the day-time.

In the end we decided to cut the honeymoon short and get back to Hong Kong. So, after fetching stores, we caught the British steamer to Wuchow, and then changed to a 'bluebottle'. The one we boarded was a wooden vessel, about ninety feet long with a powerful diesel engine that shook us passengers so much that it was difficult to read, let alone write. We were given a little cabin about five feet square, with two bunks. I suggested that Jessie should sleep on the top one, I below; but we soon found that Jessie's bunk was a highway for the rats between the hold and the kitchen. So I was to spend the nights warding off the unwelcome visitors.

In spite of the rapids, there were no accidents and we reached Nanning in safety and occupied the Chinese house we had rented, behind the hospital. Almost immediately we began to scratch and found that from head to toe, we were itching from scabies which we had caught from the river boat. The cure was for three nights, after a bath, to cover ourselves from head to toe with sulphur ointment. Eventually this did the trick.

This was the introduction to our married life in China! Perhaps it was the Lord's gentle way of showing us at the beginning what we were to expect. Despite it all we were to find that service for the Saviour was going to be a privilege and not only in China.

7

Life Together at Nanning

Soon after our wedding, when we had got back to Nanning, we welcomed Mrs Bosshardt and Mrs Hayman, whose husbands had been captured by the Red Army as it began its long trek north. In 1934, the leaders of the Communists in Kiangsi had decided to evacuate that Province and make the long march due west and then due north to North China, where they would be in closer contact with Russia. It meant crossing the provinces of Kwianghow, Kweichow, Yunnan and Szechuan. On their way through Kiangsi, they had captured the Bosshardts, and the Haymans, missionaries of the C.I.M. They released the wives, but held the husbands to ransom and compelled them to march with them, sometimes by day, sometimes by night. We did our best to provide the wives with clothes as they had lost almost everything. They were only with us a day or two before they moved elsewhere. Their husbands were to undergo that entire long march in captivity. We felt we must help as much as we were able.

Meanwhile, I was able to get a Short Term Bible School going. With the arrival of four new missionaries, Osmund Peskett, Arthur Charman, Ralph Miles and Harry Hunter, we began to think in terms of expanding the work. Two were allocated to the north, and two to the south. Gilbert Hook and his wife had already settled in Ham Chow to the south. With the countryside settling down by 1932, and brigandage lessening in the province, Mr Osborne with Ralph Miles opened up in Sheung Sz.

To the south of Nanning was the range called the 'Hundred Thousand Great Mountains'. It was a wild area, often under brigand control; Sheung Sz was a market town among the foothills. Only recently had it become safe to live there, so it was real pioneering.

Possibly through exposure to the sun, Ralph became demented and was brought back to Nanning, and it was decided that he should be sent to Hong Kong. By now there was a daily air service in small planes from Nanning to Canton. So it fell to me to escort him on the plane first to Canton and on by train to Hong Kong, not being sure that he might not become violent, but the Lord answered prayer and we got him into the Mental Hospital without trouble. It was a great grief and loss as he seemed a most promising missionary. He recovered later at home.

Our first baby, Margaret, arrived in 1936, born in the Matilda Hospital on the Peak in Hong Kong. Owing to a mistaken sense of duty, I had not gone down with Jessie, so she was on her own for the birth. I blame myself for not realizing that my primary duty should have been to be with her. However, all went well and I was able to escort her back with the baby. I had come down in the ambulance which we had acquired for the Hospital, and so was able to take them back in it. There was great interest at the Hospital in the new baby.

The evangelistic work was expanding with Ham Chow to the south occupied by the Hooks; Sheung Sz by Osborne; and Wuming by Mr Fryer and Mr Molyneux, with visits to the North. Dr Rice had returned to England by this time, but with the arrival of Dr Freda Harmer the Nanning Hospital work began to flourish again, particularly among the women patients. It was not long before we heard that the Society had received a gift of £3,000 from Miss Violet Wills for the rebuilding of the Hospital and the church at Nanning, and plans were set in motion and estimates gathered.

Meanwhile, I was beginning to feel far from well, with a grumbling appendix; I had been approached to lead a Beach Mission for the children in the China Inland Mission school in Chefoo to the north, and as Jessie had an attack of dysentery and the baby was far from well, we decided to have a holiday in North China. We booked passages on a Butterfield and Swire coastal steamer for Chefoo.

On arrival at Shanghai we discovered that the Japanese war with China had commenced and the Japanese warships were shelling the Chinese forts at Wusung outside Shanghai. Our vessel anchored in the river estuary and we waited for four days to see whether it could proceed. Meanwhile cholera broke out among the Chinese deck passengers.

A Canadian Pacific Railway's liner, the *Empress of Asia*, was evacuating women and children from Shanghai and it was decided that we should be transferred on to the *Empress of Asia* as she came down the river. There had been a mild typhoon and the river mouth was rather rough. We were put into a small rowing boat and rowed across to the great vessel as she hove to. A hatch opened in her side. Our boat was rising and falling about six or seven feet. First Jessie and the baby were manhandled through the hatch, and I followed. On getting aboard we found that there were beds and mattresses everywhere, but nowhere could we find a place to settle down. There were some 1,500 women passengers and one man beside myself! When he asked me, "Where are we going to sleep?" I replied, "I don't think it matters." Finally Jessie and I found that the first class library was unoccupied. It had a lovely thick carpet so we settled down there, and so back to Hong Kong. We were most grateful to be able to find somewhere where we could rest.

On arrival at Hong Kong it was decided that I should go into the Kowloon Hospital to have my appendix out while the baby went into the children's ward to get over infantile scurvy. Jessie was invited to stay with the Bragas in Kowloon.

While I was in Hospital, Hong Kong experienced one of its worst typhoons. Although my ward was on the inside of a quadrangle and the windows were all barred up with typhoon bars and the nurse was shouting only a foot or two away, I could not hear what she was saying. At the Bragas the bolt on the critall door had broken and Jessie struggled to keep it from flapping open in case the roof blew off.

Though in the harbour thirty two ships were blown on to the rocks, we escaped unhurt and, when we had recovered from illness, were soon able to return to Nanning, deeply grateful that the Lord had protected and provided for us.

The beginning of the war with Japan in 1937 meant that before long Canton and later, Nanning, were to be exposed to aerial attack. Air raid precautions, dugouts, and alarms began to be the order of the day.

In order to rebuild the Hospital, the running of the Outpatient Department was moved to a rented Chinese property in Yellow Mud Alley, a side street almost opposite the Hospital. This meant that no inpatients could be accepted. Jessie was helping with the treatment of patients and had to be ready to make for a dugout whenever the alarm went - with the baby, if she was at home. Many wounded by shrapnel were treated in the makeshift hospital.

A little later we were approached by the Roman Catholic French fathers as to whether it would be possible for us to transport a Catholic priest to a hospital in Hanoi. He had been wounded by shrapnel from an attack on the Catholic cathedral. "Could we take him to Hanoi in French Indo-China in our ambulance?" As the visit would enable me to visit the Chinese church in Haiphong, we agreed.

So Jessie with the little one, a year old now, and I, set out in the ambulance with a fellow priest. We made the wounded priest as comfortable as we could on the bed in the back of the ambulance. I was wearing a suit of Chinese style as the road would be very dusty. It was about 100 miles over Chinese roads before we crossed the frontier at the South Gate of China, and continued on macadam roads, changing from left hand drive to right hand. We got him safely to the hospital in Hanoi and came back to Haiphong, then a smart French city. As I prepared to change, I asked Jessie where my suit was. To her dismay she had forgotten to pack it. It was essential to be presentable and the dusty Chinese suit was out of the question. So when it became dark I went to a Chinese tailor and asked him how quickly he could make a suit. "This time tomorrow, Sir," was the answer. So in twenty four hours I had a smart new suit. It was here that my younger brother joined us from Australia where he had been teaching. He was anxious to visit our part of China and we took him back in the ambulance to Nanning.

At last the new hospital and church were completed and it was possible to accept inpatients and outpatients. The evangelistic bands, voluntary bands formed after the Bethel Band Mission (Chinese evangelists from Shanghai), were still going out and the 'hardy evangelists' continued to open up new centres of light to the south. Mr Fryer continued his trips to the north from Mo Meng.

It had been arranged that to fit in a furlough together, we should go on leave in 1938. That would mean that Jessie would have done five years and I another spell of four years. Japanese air attacks on the Canton delta meant that it was wiser not to take the usual route down the West River to Wuchow and so by steamer to Hong Kong, as shipping was being bombed. So Dr John Webb, who had arrived to assist Dr Harmer in the hospital, decided to drive us in the ambulance to Kwang Chow Waan, the French port on the South China coast, and we could get a coastal steamer there for Hong Kong. He wanted Jessie to lie on the bed in the ambulance, as she was expecting our second child, but she found that sitting was much less trying than lying on the bed. We spent the night in a Chinese temple near the French port, and eventually booked on a small coastal steamer. It proved to be a trying experience with a cargo of ducks, chickens and pigs. I wrote in my diary ...'Hardly slept all night and felt rotten, whiffs of pig, chicken, cows, opium and garlic!'

However, after a couple of days we reached Hong Kong and booked on a German liner, the *Gneisenau*. By this time the Nazi attitude was beginning to be felt and we noticed this with the ship's staff, who gave distinctive preference to German passengers, for example. We were to disembark at Genoa and go by train to Boulogne.

In the month of July, we were back in England, met by Jessie's father and taken to his vicarage in Hastings. The baby was due in August. We arranged with my doctor brother in Stoke Newington to stay with them and for Jessie to go into the Mildmay Hospital for the birth.

Meanwhile the Lord had more and more been laying on my heart the needs of the country folk, the 'earth' people as the Chinese called them. By this time I knew that they were of Thai stock and that there were some ten millions of them in our province and that no one had tried to reach them in their own language, as their own dialects seemed to vary a good deal from place to place. But for some years nothing developed beyond praying for these people.

Meanwhile, with the growth of Nazi influence in Germany, the threat of World War Two was looming. War clouds seemed to lower at the B.C.M.S. Annual Meeting in September 1938, but with the phoney agreement between Chamberlain and Hitler, the tension eased for some eight months.

As tension grew again, we moved from my mother's house in Parkstone to Jessie's parents at Whinburgh in Norfolk. It was while there that, on Sunday morning, Mr Kitley had arranged that at 11.00 am his wife would come into church after listening to the news and raise her hand if we were at war again. We made a room gas proof and did one or two other preparations, but as hostilities did not really begin, we asked to go back to the work in China. With a family we were not allowed to sail through the Suez Canal, but embarked on an American liner for New York, planning to cross the States by coach and sail from Vancouver to Hong Kong.

36 hours after leaving Southampton in November 1939, I got up in the morning to see land on both sides of the vessel. We were sailing up the river on our way to Bordeaux. Before long we arrived at Bordeaux and there, though we did not know it, took on France's gold reserves.

We were welcomed by the British Council in New York, had a week in New Jersey, and then caught the coach to Chicago. As it was considered impossible to take two small children by coach all the way, we took the train at Chicago and travelled to Seattle and Vancouver. It was certainly much easier for Jessie to cope with feeding the children on the train, instead of only a quarter of an hour stop on the coach. So the Lord had overruled our plan to our great relief. I was amazed how calmly Jessie coped with all the changing conditions that we were experiencing. We crossed the Rockies at Whitefish and so down to Seattle and Vancouver.

We had hoped to spend a week in Vancouver, but found that the *Empress of Russia* was sailing for Hong Kong the next day. To save money for the Society we booked a cabin in steerage, but on getting there we found that the approach to the cabins in steerage was by a sort of glorified ladder and when we got into the cabin, Jessie's heart sank. The partition between the cabins left a gap of one foot above the floor. One side of the cabin was the metal side of the ship. A cold blast blew between the cabins at floor level. It would be impossible to sit the baby on the floor. Even Jessie's calm was shaken.

I climbed up onto the third class deck and found there was an empty cabin there and approached the ship's purser. He agreed to let us move up there, but said it would be occupied after Honolulu. So, deeply thankful for the Lord's provision, we went a deck above. In the steerage there were in fact no comfortable chairs or anywhere to sit down. On the deck to which we had come, we found a party of China Inland missionaries so we had fellowship with them and at least the baby could sit on the cabin floor. At Honolulu no one came to take the cabin, so we had it right through to Hong Kong, deeply grateful to our Heavenly Father and a great relief to Jessie.

At Yokohama we were told there was to be a compulsory medical examination on the upper deck. The baby had a cold so we begged to have her examined somewhere indoors. "No, you must appear on the top deck," they said, in bitterly cold weather. By the evening she was gasping for breath with incipient pneumonia. However, the Lord came to our help. The ship's doctor ordered her to be transferred to the ship's hospital and immediately her breathing eased. We wondered if we should have to break the journey at Shanghai and take her to hospital, but by the time we reached Shanghai she was well again, and there was no need.

8

Evacuation to Burma and
Return to Nanning

Unfortunately, on arrival in Hong Kong, we found that the Japanese army had already occupied the Nanning area and it was no longer possible to go back there. However, there was a big job to be done in Hong Kong as the Orphanage was to be moved to the New Territories, so this occupied my time. In the meantime a new doctor, John Webb, had begun work at the Hospital. He and Herbert Osborne were in Nanning, but could get across the frontier into what was then French Indo-China and John's mother had possession of a house at Chapa in a hill resort in Indo-China. We could get there from Hong Kong by sea, so it was decided to hold a Conference of South China missionaries at Chapa for a week and make plans for the future. Freda Poskett, Marjorie Hook and Jessie were left. All three wives were pregnant. So, with the children in Hong Kong, the husbands made their way to Chapa.

About the middle of the week news came through that France had made peace with the Germans and British troops were being evacuated from Dunkirk. The French in Vietnam turned anti-British, so we made full speed to get back to Hong Kong. Japanese troops were already landing at Haiphong as we passed through and took the first boat to Hong Kong. On arrival, we were met by three tearful wives, informing us that they had been ordered to sail for Australia on the next day. Jessie was disturbed by the idea of herself with the two children arriving in Australia with no husband and expecting the arrival of another little one. It must have been a frightening prospect for her.

We were not at all in favour of going to Australia, so we prayed about it; we felt that we would much rather go to Burma where

B.C.M.S. had extensive work in the north, and where there would be Chinese amongst whom we could do some active missionary work. We were given permission and caught a B.I. steamer for Rangoon. Jessie had the two older children and was in her sixth month.

After leaving Singapore we were startled by hearing a very loud explosion which might well have brought on Jessie's pregnancy. It turned out that, without warning the passengers, they had fitted a four inch gun on the stern of the ship and they were trying this out! However, we did not suffer.

On arrival at Rangoon we went to see the famous pagoda, the Shwee Dagon. This was a Buddhist shrine, faced in gold, of about 300 feet high and was visible from the Irawaddy River. Then we went to the Deaf and Dumb home and prepared for the railway journey to Mandalay, and then on to Mohnyin, where B.C.M.S. had opened a hospital.

A railway ran from Rangoon to Myitkina in the far north, and passed through Mohnyin. The Irawaddy River flowed past Mohnyin, on to Mandalay, and so down to Rangoon and the coast. From Mandalay there was an evangelistic outreach amongst the different language groups, Burmese, Shan, Jinghpaw, to the headhunting Nagas further north. Around Mohnyin there was a thick jungle. A jam among the teak logs floating down the river would mean that elephants were brought in to find out where the jam was and remove it. It was fascinating to watch these elephants at work.

The Burmese and Shans were Buddhists. The Jinghpaw were spirit worshippers and petrified of evil spirits. So there was a great deal of evangelizing to be done.

Mandalay was the local government centre for central Burma. It was then a walled town and contained the old palace, built from finely carved hardwoods, and a fine sight in the town centre. It had been the old Royal Palace. We were surprised to find that amongst the Burmese, the women did the work in the fields; the men remained at home, generally smoking their cheroots.

We stayed with an old Society for the Propagation of the Gospel missionary, a bachelor who had worked there for many years. He was at a loss how to entertain the children. We then took the train to Mohnyin and were welcomed into the Rushton's home. Jessie had stood the journey well and we were so thankful to our Heavenly Father that now we could settle down again to missionary work.

We were told that we would need four or five servants. Because of the caste system in Burma, the water carrier, of one caste, would not be allowed to sweep and the cook, of a different caste again would not be allowed to carry water, and so on. On a China missionary's salary to employ a number of servants would have been impossible but we managed to find a Chinese man who would do all or any of the jobs.

We were now in a Mandarin speaking area, the Chinese being from Yunnan in West China, so Jessie found that the Mandarin she had learned, and what I had learned in England, was now to be useful. My custom was to go into the Chinese eating house and get into conversation and introduce the gospel.

In one of these, I noticed a Chinese cook with the most miserable face I had ever seen. After I had gone there once or twice, he came across and listened to what was being said. The next time he came across, and when I had finished, he asked me, "Can Jesus save an opium smoker?" I replied, "Yes, would you like to come and talk about it?" So that evening he came and we talked about the Christian faith, that there is one God, the Creator, who loves us, Christ who came to die for our sins and to save us, the possibility of a new Birth, a free gift to be received. Would he like to receive it and ask for forgiveness and a new heart? He said "Yes," so we knelt down and, for the first time in his life, he prayed and asked for God's forgiveness. Later he came for treatment in the Hospital.

Some two or three weeks later I had an invitation to take the train to Mo Guang and preach to the Chinese community there. There must have been some two hundred present. So, in stumbling Mandarin I preached the Gospel. After we had finished, a man came up to me. "Do you remember me?" he asked. I said, "No, I'm afraid

I don't." "I'm the opium smoker." His face had changed completely. It was he, I understood, who had arranged the gathering.

Another interesting experience in Mohnyin was being approached by a Chinese business man, Mr Chang, who wanted to become a Christian. I asked him if he understood what it meant. "No," he replied. He wanted to become a Christian because of what he had seen in T'eng Yueh over the Chinese border. Mr Chang once saw a missionary carrying a sick Chinese carrier on his back. He had found him at the side of the road and had carried him on his back seven miles into the town. "A religion which will make a man do that, I want as my religion." So I was able to prepare him for baptism later on. It was J.O. Frazer who was the missionary.

So the Lord had opened a door of opportunity for us in Upper Burma. Jessie, after I left, was able haltingly to hold a little Bible class in their house, and the man who had come as our servant was brought to the Lord and baptized.

While we were there our third daughter, Rachel, was born and we had a happy baptism in the little church there.

After we had been in Burma for three months, we got the news that the Japanese had pulled out of our part of China and at the same time came the news that Mr Churchill had allowed the Burma Road into China to be reopened. As it became clear that I could get back over the Burma road, it must have been a very severe test of Jessie's faith to agree to my going and leaving her and the children behind, without knowing when she might see me again, but she faced it willingly and encouraged me to go. With her full approval I and Victor Dixon, a new missionary, decided that we would attempt to get permission to travel on Chinese Army lorries, starting from Lashio in the Shan States.

How long it would take and how much we should have to pay we did not know, but we felt it was worth having a go to get back to our work. If it was felt wise and safe, Jessie and the family might follow later. She felt she would like to make the attempt. I waved goodbye to Jessie and the three children and committed them into the Lord's hands, having no idea when we would see each other again.

After saying my goodbyes to our very kind missionary friends in Burma, I made my way by rail to Mandalay and then by rail again to Lashio. On arrival I went to the offices of the South Western Transportation Company and saw their official. "Could we book for two to travel to Nanning over the Burma Road on your lorries?" "Yes," he said, "that can be arranged." So he issued the two tickets, bits of paper in Chinese. "How much will that be?" I asked. "Oh, I don't think that we need to make any charge," he replied.

So the Lord had arranged that we could get back to China without charge. I was most surprised and deeply grateful to our Heavenly Father. He had made it possible just at the right time for the Burma Road to be reopened after being closed for a year or more and for us to be able to get permission to go on the army lorries. So we praised the Lord and took courage. We had no idea what it would involve.

As the Japanese armies had pushed westward and had closed all the seaports in China, it became essential to find a way to supply the Chinese armies with military equipment and so, with American assistance, Chiang Kai Shek planned to make a road, later called the Burma Road, that could be used to send the arms and other supplies needed into China. It was a Herculean task for the mountain ranges lay north and south, and the road ran west to east. In addition, there were two of the world's longest rivers (the Mekong and the Salween) which had to be crossed. Suspension bridges had to be built on both rivers - in the case of the Salween, some two or three hundred feet across, and consisting of two chains with thick board fastened on them crosswise. It spanned the river some two hundred feet above the water level.

From the Burmese frontier to Kunming, the road passed through only three or four sizeable towns, but it also passed through one of the world's worst malarial spots, the Shweli and Salween valleys. So bad was the reputation of these valleys that travellers made every effort to hasten across them before sunset, their scarves held over their mouths to keep out the 'evil' air - their eyes averted from the yellow apparitions like the one we saw.

He was a young man of corpse-like appearance. His face was greyish-black and what had been the whites of his eyes was literally and actually green. As we approached, he turned those horrible eyes on us, with a dazed and other-worldly motion that was ghastly. This people attributed the illness to their being possessed with devils who, they maintained, came punctually every second or third day.

At times the road would rise and fall some three to four thousand feet as each range was crossed. Sometimes it had to be made on the saddle of steep mountain ranges with declines of two or three thousand feet on either side. Occasionally they had to blast through stone cliffs which overhung the road and with a drop of several hundred feet at the side. In very few parts was there any side wall to the road. The road track often consisted of ruts a foot deep; sometimes clouds of red dust rose as the lorries went over it. All petrol had to be carried in fifty gallon drums; none was available on the road. In parts there was the danger of brigands.

The scenery was magnificent, in places really tropical, in others barely temperate. At one point we approached what appeared to be a steep mountainside, and proceeded to climb it by means of twenty-four hairpin bends; many abandoned lorries could be seen at the roadside.

From the Burmese frontier into mid-China was a distance of fifteen hundred miles, and the road - completed in 1938 - was almost entirely built and maintained by hand labour. Several thousand Chinese workmen died in building it. But so bad had the road become in 1941 that Churchill had it closed for a year. It was only after drying off and extensive repairs that it was reopened just before we attempted it.

When the time came to leave Lashio, we climbed into the cabin of a lorry and travelled through the Shan States and crossed the China border. I think it was the first night over the border when we stopped in Meng She. We had passed the International Malaria Research Station near the malarial area. If I remember rightly we spent the night in a school and without mosquito nets, but neither of us caught anything. It was not long the next day before we reached

63

the Salween bridge. It was single track, and only one lorry at a time could cross in either direction. We noticed that the brick built towers were showing cracks owing to Japanese bombing and the railings on one side or another were missing in places, but slowly and carefully the driver took us across. It was with a sigh of relief that we mounted the other side and began to ascend.

On this road there were many hazards and we could see several abandoned lorries which had gone off the road. On one occasion we were ascending the part of the road which ran on the saddle of a mountain with steep slopes of something like 2000 feet on either side. There were no walls or edges. As we ascended, the engines suddenly stalled. We were sitting on the cargo behind the cabin. Dixon jumped off as we began to roll backwards, but the driver managed to get the engine started again, and I had the laugh over Dixon.

We crossed the Mekong on the newly constructed suspension bridge; the old chain bridge, built more than a thousand years earlier, ran parallel to it.

The views were often quite breathtaking. Without going into Ta Li we got a magnificent view of the very large lake, the Erh Hai at whose side Ta Li was built. Behind it rose the snow covered peak of the Tien Tsang Mountain, with the pagodas and houses of Ta Li nestling at its foot.

On the last day, the seventeenth of our journey, the only lorry we could find going to Nanning was loaded with high explosives; so we had to take it and were seated on the boxes of explosives behind the driver's cabin. We had been going some time when suddenly we saw another lorry approaching. The driver swerved, but struck a glancing blow on the side of the other lorry. We did not stop, but a pain in my little finger made me aware that the metal strut to support the tarpaulin in wet weather had been sheered off and had come down on my little finger and broken it. In spite of treatment by Doctor Webb, it is still deformed to this day! Had I not had on my leather gloves it would have been cut off. So we thanked God that nothing worse had happened. We might well have been killed or blown up.

The Lord had watched over us throughout the journey which might have ended so differently. Our hearts were deeply grateful.

We found that with the Japanese withdrawal, things were fairly quiet and we could carry on the work of training Chinese leaders and getting the gaps filled; one promising young worker had been shot by the Japanese. John Webb and Herbert Osborne, who had stayed through the Japanese occupation, had been given an American relief lorry and they felt that they needed a change. So as it seemed alright for Jessie and the family to come back, they decided to take the lorry to Burma (Hong Kong was already in the hands of the Japanese) and have a holiday there and then with a metal cover fixed to the lorry base, bring Jessie and the family back with them. Dixon and I would carry on in Nanning.

9

Jessie on the Burma Road

Jessie writes, 'God sent us a very faithful Chinese cook. How well I remember holding the little Bible readings round our dining room table, trying to speak in Mandarin and getting the meaning over to them in halting words. Perhaps this was the reason for the seemingly wasted time in those early days in learning Mandarin before turning to Cantonese. Later this Chinese servant was baptized.'

On receiving the news that she was to come back to Nanning, she began to prepare, a very brave decision, to make the journey with three small children, one a baby. The journey would be in March and would involve a train journey to Mandalay on her own; a taxi drive up into the Shan States without being able to speak the language, and then the journey, fifteen hundred miles, over the Burma Road, without knowing what provisions were needed for the journey. But there was no hesitation in her mind. She would face it. She writes, 'Perhaps God was preparing even then for such an eventuality as this? Now the summons came in the New Year to set out on this unknown journey along the Burma Road with three small children, Rachel being only seven months old. How I sympathized with Abraham "who went out not knowing whither he went". But God was with him and he was going to be with us, and so we prepared, not knowing very much of the problems ahead and with no one to consult who had been over it before us. We purchased some essential tinned food, dried milk and porridge oats for the children and set off in March on the great adventure. We were to meet Dr Webb and Mr Osborne in Lashio. They had come out from Nanning for a rest after their internment there.

'I set off by train with the three children to Mandalay with enough food for the journey. I had to tie a cord on to the two children, while

66

feeding the baby, as the compartment windows could not be shut. In Mandalay I managed to get a car to take us the last stage of the journey by road to Maymyo. This was rather an undertaking as I could not speak Burmese and my driver could speak hardly any English; however, we arrived safely after winding up and up through beautiful tropical scenery on all sides. Tremendous bends in the road made the children sick and made me feel very uncomfortable. So we were rather a woebegone party when we arrived at the comfortable American Rest House, but soon felt better when we were cared for by kind friends of the American Mission. We stayed there for about three weeks until finally the lorry was ready and we prepared to set out on our long trek to Kwangsi, travelling first by train to Lashio. It was hard to leave the comfort of the Mission House, and comparative civilization for a journey that was bound to be difficult and dangerous and full of strange experiences. But when God sends one forth, He also gives the grace and promise of his presence, "all the days".'

For Jessie, travelling over the Burma Road with three small children must have been a very real test of faith, with the possibility of accidents, brigands, or the uncertainty of what lay ahead at the back of her mind.

'We were a small party, three lady missionaries, a doctor, a clergyman, three small children and a Chinese driver from our Hospital in Nanning. We spent the first night in a small school where we spread our bedding on the iron bedsteads in a dormitory. After a wash and supper, we slept fitfully until morning when our journey really began.

'We were to sleep in varied conditions; it is impossible to mention them all. I think the greatest contrast was from the comfort of Maymyo to the second night of our journey, when we had expected to sleep in one of the Government Rest Houses, dotted along the road, only to find it was full and we were led to the annexe (which sounded wonderful) but was in reality a few mat sheds with wooden bed boards and a mud floor, and one rough wooden table and two small forms for our dining room. Here we slept and made our meals with a primus stove.

Later we moved into the Rest House where at least we were able to get hot water and a wash.

'We stayed one night at the Malarial Research Station, shut in with wire mosquito netting.

'Often we ate our meals at wayside inns, Chinese food, of course. We were able to obtain rice gruel and eggs for the children. It was safe from flies as it was well boiled. We could also quench our thirst with Chinese tea, kept boiling in huge cauldrons for passing visitors to the inn. The Chinese food was supplemented by cakes and biscuits brought with us. Fruit we bought at the markets.

'Sometimes we slept in Chinese inns overrun with rats and other vermin, but wherever we could, we stayed with missionaries in stations on our route. What a joy to get really clean and enjoy fellowship in Christ with one another. We always tried to do this at weekends, so that we might have opportunities for worship and spend the day quietly.

'We planned to leave at break of day, after a cup of coffee and some porridge, filling up the thermos flasks with boiling water to make up the baby's bottles on the way. To each one was given a special job to see to, so that all would go smoothly on the way. We normally stopped at some market town on the way about 10.00 am for our Chinese 'breakfast' and then set off, trying to arrive at our objective before dark, but when delayed it sometimes meant staying in the lorry for me and the children as they would already be asleep. Our Chinese driver faithfully guarded us in the driver's seat while we slept. We had a bunk fitted across the front of the lorry behind the driver's seat with two seats on either side, so that it was possible to take it in turns to rest or put the children to sleep while we journeyed. The only way out was to climb over the bonnet of the lorry. Behind us was our luggage and huge drums of petrol to take us to the next available depot.

"We often stopped for a snack by the wayside amidst beautiful scenery. We washed nappies in a wayside mountain stream and hung them up in the lorry to dry, sitting on them afterwards to air them. It was rather primitive, but in spite of all the difficulties, God kept us from any serious illness on the way. Sometimes our route led us over dangerous mountain passes, chain bridges over the Mekong and

Salween rivers that swayed and creaked as we crossed them (they had recently been bombed and in many places were just planks laid on the chains). Sometimes our way led us through brigand-infested country, when it was unwise to stop on the way. But a Heavenly Father preserved us through it all.

'We spent a night in an old temple in Paoshan used as an inn, and then a weekend at Ta Li, a beautiful city by the lake, passing through the red dusty plain of Tali from Hsia Kuan. Here we stayed the weekend at the C.I.M. Station and spent most of it trying to get rid of the red dust which covered us from head to toe and penetrated all our luggage. I saw very little of the beauties of Ta Li. My remembrances are mostly of a series of cauldrons with clothes boiling in them and lines and lines of washing hung up to dry. By Monday we were clean and ready to start off again, saying "goodbye" to our kind friends who made us so welcome.

'We passed through beautiful scenery as we approached Kweichow, the sides of the mountains covered in the most beautiful flowers and shrubs. A stay in an inn in this province stands out in memory, a province where the people rarely wash. The little town had been heavily bombed, but amongst the ruins was this dirty old inn. Beggars can't be choosers, so here we unpacked our things to stay the night. The food was not tempting and sanitary arrangements most primitive, as they were all along the journey. We unpacked bedding and tried to settle for the night. Rachel was in her basket on the bed with the children, and I was on another. In the night I heard her cry out and got up to attend to her and found a rat had been nibbling her face. No more sleep for me. We all got on the same bed and I spent the rest of the night on guard to keep the marauders at bay.

'One weekend we spent at Pan Hsien, a C.I.M. Station where the Bosshardts normally lived. The house being empty, all the pasted paper windows were broken; several of us slept, or tried to, in one big bed and lay and shivered in the piercing north wind that was blowing. Still it was comparatively comfortable and the ladies made soup and cooked some good nourishing food. We were able to worship with the Chinese Christians in a nearby church.

'Another time, we arrived later than usual at the gates of a city where we expected to spend the night with the C.I.M. Missionaries. We found the gates locked and no amount of persuasion would induce the soldiers to open them, so we had to stay in the lorry with no supper apart from a little porridge which we gave to the children. How we welcomed a good breakfast prepared for us when we got into the city at 5.00 am!

'At last, on Easter Sunday, April 12, just three weeks after leaving Burma, we came in sight of Nanning. What a welcome awaited us. How glad we were of the hot baths prepared for us and how we thanked God for all his care of us on the journey!'

Jessie continues, 'After a stay in the Hospital, we later moved to a large Chinese building on the outskirts of Nanning, which was rented for a Bible School. Here we occupied the top floor with a lovely view overlooking the aerodrome. The students lived below. Before long we began to be subjected to repeated bombings from the Japanese air force and life became rather complicated and it was not easy to carry on consecutive teaching in the Bible School.

'In January, 1942, Rosemary, our fourth, arrived. In the middle of all this, when she was four days old, there was a severe bombing of a part of Nanning and I and the baby had to take refuge under a bed on the ground floor, but God preserved us and each time we were able to get to the dug-out with the children.

'Before Rosemary's arrival, Mr Charman, while living with us, went down with typhus and was very ill. I nursed him for awhile and then it was thought wiser to move him to Hospital.'

10

Evacuation to India and Return to England

The previous chapter was Jessie's account, now I resume the story.

While we were in the Bible School, we experienced a severe flood. Normally the West River would rise in the summer some 80 feet but, with continuous rain, it spread over the flat areas and over the banks. At last it reached our house and, as it was still rising, it was felt wise to transfer the family to the Hospital on higher ground. I decided to take down the very large wooden doors, which were detachable, and use one to ferry the family to higher ground. Outside the house the path was about seven feet wide and passed through rice fields. This path was under water to a depth of three or four feet, the rice fields a foot or two lower. The difficulty was that after some twenty yards of straight the path turned at right angles and led to higher ground. It was impossible with one wide sheet of water to see where the path was, or where the bend was, and a false step here or on either side would cause us to be out of our depth.

However, having placed Jessie and the baby on the door and floated it out, with the help of a bamboo rod, I was able to push the door with its precious cargo forward, feeling with the bamboo rod for the side of the path and, when we got there, the bend in the path. Having landed them safely, I returned for the three children and followed the same pattern though with the bamboo rod now stuck in at the bend so that I knew where I was. So the whole family was safely provided for in the Hospital. During this episode we found that Audrey had been bitten on the heel by a snake which was floating on the water. Unfortunately I had not seen what kind of snake, so I sucked the wound thoroughly and there were no ill effects. Again, we were so grateful for our Heavenly Father's protection in this emergency.

We had, in the Bible School, some ten students and it looked as if this would be our main work in the immediate future, but it was not to be. At that time the Chinese dollar was pegged to the pound, and it was steadily losing its value with the result that to accept merely a salary that would cover our food and necessities required a very large sum from the Society. So it was finally decided that, since our large family was the heaviest drain on Mission funds, we should be evacuated.

The American Air Force, whose planes came occasionally from Yunnan, offered to fly us to Kunming, from where we could take a China National Aviation Corporation plane to Calcutta. So we began to sell what possessions we had, including wedding presents, as we had no idea whether it would be possible to return. Since Hong Kong had fallen, the Japanese were in control of Burma and most of east Asia.

On arrival in Kunming we found that as the Japanese were shooting down planes by day, we would be flying at night and blacked out. We were told to wear our thickest winter clothing as we should be flying at 20,000 feet over the hump in a Dakota, if I remember rightly, without air conditioning. So it was a case of just trusting ourselves and our little ones into the Heavenly Father's hands to take care of us and he did not let us down. We came down at 4.00 am at Dinapur in Assam, and arrived at Calcutta at Dum Dum aerodrome, at 6.00 am, still in our thick winter clothing. When we got to the Hotel for breakfast, everyone else was in white; our faces were red as beetroots.

Where were we to stay? It had been impossible to make any arrangements. In trepidation, we went to the vicarage of the Old Mission church, connected with Henry Martyn, a well known missionary in India. After announcing ourselves, four children and another expected, the vicar asked me if we stayed there, whether my wife be spending the day in bed. I assured him she would not, and we were welcomed in. It turned out that a missionary family with two small boys had left the Westcotts to look after the children while the mother kept to her bed! Prices in Calcutta seemed very low after China. We had, through selling all we had, accumulated a little cash reserve and the children were thrilled to be able to buy new dolls and have some new clothes.

In connection with the Old Mission Church, there was a Chinese speaking congregation. Owing to disagreements, it had dwindled until it barely survived. I was able, with Jessie's help, to get it started again. We had a prayer meeting and cups of tea, and soon it began to grow. One day I noticed in the congregation a man in fine silks and got talking to him afterwards. It turned out that he was a Tibetan named Jamba Wosel, a tea merchant who travelled between Lhasa and Calcutta. His mother was Cantonese so he spoke Chinese as well as Tibetan. He became interested and later was baptized, so perhaps my early interest in Tibet was not wholly lost. The congregation slowly built up and after we left and another ex-China missionary assisted, I heard it had grown to some 200 people. So God had been leading and took us to help them just at the right time.

After some six weeks we reluctantly said "goodbye" to the Westcotts who had been such good friends and took the train for the United Provinces where the B.C.M.S. had work for us to do. In the United Provinces I played a game of cricket for the Christians against the Muslims. I can't recall who won! It was intriguing to pass over the Ganges at Benares and see passengers throw coins into the sacred river.

We were met by a bullock cart and car to take us to the B.C.M.S Hospital at Kachwa, half way between Benares and Allahabad. There Dr Everard's skill as a surgeon was attracting large numbers of patients. We were intrigued to see on the open ground in front of the Hospital little groups of patients round fires, cooking food for their particular caste.

While there, our fifth daughter, Joan, was born in January 1944. I vividly remember walking with Jessie over the *maidan* to the ladies' bungalow after she had started in labour.

A day or two later, I went out with an evangelistic team on the sacred road round Benares. On our return Jessie told me that a message had come that there was a ship sailing for home from Bombay in a few days' time. Did we want to book passages on it? Jessie had still not got up after the birth, and I left it entirely in her hands to decide whether we should or should not accept the passage. After talking it over, she decided that we should accept and got up to begin the packing and getting ready to leave. The baby, Joan, was baptized in the little church in Kachwa before we left.

In a day or so we caught the train for Bombay and were taken to the P.& O. liner. There we learnt that on the voyage we would be separated, Jessie with the children in one part of the ship, I in another. We hesitated and prayed about it. Finally Jessie said "Yes", and we boarded the vessel only to find that Jessie, the four children and the baby, a mother with two small children and an old lady would be in one cabin; I in another part of the ship. Life jackets, including a special one for the baby, must be carried wherever we went, on deck, in the cabins, at meals. It seemed an impossible situation, but after one night, the ship's doctor stepped in and said we must be given a cabin to ourselves. So from then on we were together. Again the Lord had graciously provided for us and met our apparently insurmountable difficulties.

While standing on the deck, I noticed that the shadows were changing and that we had turned at right angles. Looking in the direction we had been travelling, I saw on the horizon a column of smoke going up; Japanese submarines had got an oil tanker. However, when we entered the Red Sea things got a little easier. We passed through the Suez canal, although the Germans still occupied Crete. But in the Mediterranean, owing to the number of mines, the convoy proceeded single file, until we passed Gibraltar. Then we nearly touched the United States coast before turning east.

I was struck by Jessie's coolness and patience when, for nearly five weeks she had to look after children, watch the life jackets, care for the baby, make sure that they were happy and comfortable. A sea voyage with children is never easy; under those conditions it could have been a nightmare.

When we reached Northern Ireland, we began to drop depth charges in case there were submarines. A day or two before reaching our destination, Audrey went down with measles and we were confined to the cabin. At last, we anchored at Gourock and the passengers disembarked, but we were asked to wait while Audrey was taken to the isolation hospital and preparations made for us to be taken to the W.V.S. centre in Glasgow.

The Glasgow W.V.S. could not have been more thoughtful and caring. They took the children under their care and relieved my wife of the baby. They served us with a splendid meal, followed by a rest and then had us driven down to the station and led us past a 200 yards queue to a reserved compartment in the southbound train. They could not have been kinder.

On arrival at Wymondham station in Norfolk we were met by Jessie's father with the car. All the children were in tears with incipient measles. But we had a warm welcome at Whinburgh Rectory where he was Vicar. Jessie's mother soon had them all in bed and our long journey, nearly six weeks from India, was at last completed. Again our Heavenly Father had kept us and provided for us in so many way.

11

Parish Life and College Life in England

A friend of mine, the Reverend Harris, who was a Vicar at Cranwell in Suffolk, knew of a parish nearby which was desperately in need of an incumbent. I went to visit it and soon after was installed as Rector of Bedingfield, which was a small country parish. It was still a case of wartime austerity, rationing and occasional air raids, doodlebugs and flying bombs. Once a flying bomb exploded some three miles away and the glass doors opening on the lawn, though locked, burst wide open. Jessie was lent a pony and trap and used to drive the four or five miles into Eye for shopping or sometimes would cycle ten miles into Diss, a large market town.

It was while we were at Bedingfield in 1945 that Christopher was born. Jessie could hardly believe it when she was told that it was a boy. He was three weeks late.

It was at Bedingfield that we heard at last that Germany had capitulated - V.E. Day - though the war still continued with Japan in the Far East.

It was while at Bedingfield that I made what was perhaps the greatest mistake of my life. Without praying over it or seeking the Lord's guidance, I registered to take a PhD at London University, taking as a subject a Chinese history of a kingdom in Yunnan Province. It improved my Chinese and was connected with the tribal people to whom I had felt drawn in South China, but I am sure it was not the Lord's will.

After some eighteen months, I was asked to join the Reverend Dodgson Sykes, Principal of the Bible Churchmen's Missionary Training College in Bristol, as Vice Principal. So our time in Bedingfield was very short, but perhaps something had been done among the children.

For example one of the choir girls, Pamela Harvey, subsequently became a deaconess.

So we settled at the College. I was lecturing for the most part on the New Testament, and Jessie was starting the children with reading and writing, and was looking after the baby.

In the August, I was studying the history of Yunnan in Cambridge University Library. It was small Chinese print and required a great deal of close work and concentration and I got to the point where I realized I had overdone things and found that I could not sleep for weeks on end. We tried a holiday in the Doone Valley in Devon. I can remember getting up in the middle of the night quite unable to sleep. What made things worse was a deep fear that I should lose my reason. As I stood by the window and looked out, I told the Lord that I was willing for His Will, whatever it might cost, and from then very slowly I began to relax, but it was still not possible to read without getting a bad headache. Nor could I lecture. Jessie was wonderful and stood by me without commiserating. This continued until about November. Then to my amazement I got a letter from the Society suggesting we should return to China. I had just about written myself off, but this created a new hope and I began to get better quickly. Passages were booked on a liner, as now the Japanese war had ended. The students came to see us off on the train; Christopher was almost left behind as one of the students was holding him when the train was about to start. Slowly the Lord restored my health in spite of my mistake and I began to be able to use my brain again.

On arrival in Hong Kong in 1946, I was able to free myself from the job of Mission Secretary and to begin to concentrate on the language of the country people. It was decided then that instead of living in Nanning, we should occupy the house in Wu Ming, thirty miles further north, a centre of the tribal folk, the Zhuang, in order to learn the language and reach these people.

Mo Ming (or in Mandarin, Wu Ming) was a large market town with markets every three days. It had been the home of the Governor of the Province, General Luk Wing Ting. It was a special beauty spot with stone mountains all around and a river coming out of the rock formation in the park called Ling Shui - 'Spirit Water'. The population all around were Zhuang and on market days it was the Zhuang language that could be heard.

In Nanning before moving to Wu Ming we nearly lost Rachel. In the garden of the Asiatic Petroleum Company where we were having tea there was a cesspit with a wooden cover over the round opening. The wood was rotten and Rachel, chasing a kitten, walked on it. It gave way and Rachel clung by her hands as she hung over the cesspit edge. A Chinese boy helped her. Rosemary ran to us crying, "Rachel is gone." We dashed round and gently pulled her out, just in time.

We had left the two elder girls in England at Clarendon School in Abergele, hoping that as soon as the C.I.M. School reopened they would come out and be at school there. However, the Chinese Communist offensive in the north made it impossible to reopen it. So our hopes were dashed and they had to remain in England.

By the time we had got up country, it was clear that nothing was going to hold the Communists back. Nevertheless we went to Wu Ming only to find that the house, a long building with two storeys, had been bombed and only the rooms at each end were still there, two in all. One room was a pigsty! We stayed in Nanning while the house was rebuilt.

In 1947 the Anglican Church in China was to hold a General Synod in Shanghai. As we were now in the Chung Hua Shing Kung Huei as an embryo missionary district, I was asked to attend and we met in the fine Girls' School there. All the Bishops were present and many clergy and laity. It was most interesting to meet the representatives from other parts of China. We had helpful Bible Studies given by Bishop Shen Tze Kao.

On the return journey by air we came down in Canton and approaching Hong Kong, ran into low cloud. We circled several times looking for a break in the clouds. Finally the pilot flew out to sea and came back not much above the masts of the ships, climbed over the saddle and came down safely. Hong Kong aerodrome was surrounded by hills, except from the sea. So it was a difficult landing.

That was not the only difficult approach I had to Hong Kong. About that time, I had to take the river boat on the way to Hong Kong. As I boarded it at Nanning, I noticed that the river was very swollen with the summer rains. The duck board that ran along the side of the vessel was only an inch or so above the river. We were to call in at Nam Heung on the right hand side of the river. As we approached in the darkness, the pilot turned the vessel too sharply and being flat bottomed, we heeled over sharply. I saw a soldier standing on the duck board with water up to his knees. All the passengers crowded towards the right hand side to see what it was. This meant that it heeled over even further. I held my breath for if it had capsized we should all have been drowned like rats in a cage. Gradually it righted itself and we regained an upright position. How grateful I was that once again we had been protected and cared for.

Back in Wu Ming I spent the mornings with a language teacher, a Zhuang, and helping at times in the church, where there was a Chinese pastor. Jessie had, at last, got just the work she loved, holding a clinic in a little side building each morning with a blind Zhuang woman to interpret and to explain the gospel to the patients while they waited. Jessie began taking midwifery calls as they came, the number increasing as her skill became known in the district round. She writes:

'We also opened a small, but very primitive midwifery ward. Here, gradually, the country folk began to find help in their time of need and many of them for the first time after years of sorrow took home a live baby. An old blind woman used to come and talk to the patients in their own language and we were able to show a little of the love of Christ to these needy people. God wonderfully answered prayer, time and time again, and often, alone and unaided, especially at night God seemed just to take hold of one's hands, feeble as they were, and often trembling, and work through them. Here, too, we experienced God's care and protection, twice finding a cobra, one curled up in the dark kitchen and another in the nursery.'

In August 1948 we had a conference to discuss the imminent prospect of a Communist takeover. All of us missionaries, without exception, decided to stay at our posts and see if we could continue the work. The Bishop of Hong Kong felt that in face of this decision we ought to have a good holiday as we had no idea when another might be possible. He chartered the Lutheran plane and flew us to Hong Kong. While there, our seventh child, Jill, was born. On our return, we were loaded with provisions that might not be available. These were given by the Hong Kong diocese.

We had decided that in view of the possibility of fighting, we would leave the two older children in Hong Kong with the Mulrenans. In spite of a mistake by the Bishop in not registering them at the School, the Lord enabled them to be accepted and we could return inland knowing that they would be well cared for.

The Communists were advancing steadily southwards. Everyone was in fear. We dared not trust anybody. Sons would accuse their parents, or parents their sons or daughters. There was a box into which anonymous accusations could be placed and which would be taken by the secret police. One shopkeeper told me that he had always trusted his neighbour, but now had lost all confidence in him. It was a life of constant uncertainty and fear. We determined we would stick it out as long as we could.

One Saturday night, a Christian Nationalist officer came in to say "goodbye". He had been in once or twice before. He told us that they were moving out that night and we could expect the Communist Army to come in. Jessie was able to give him her warm leather coat which enabled him to survive and reach safety.

The next day, Sunday, the local people organized a 'Home Guard' as no Communist army had arrived. The service was at noon. I was taking the service and wondered if I ought to pray for Chiang Kai Shek or Mao Tze Tung. Going into the back garden after the service, we found the head of a cow, thrown over from the Government premises behind, and a mass of unused rifle bullets. We felt it would not be wise for the Communists, when they came, to find these on our premises. So I wrapped them in a newspaper and threw them back. Then I remembered it was an English newspaper, so had to fish it back again.

I got a long bamboo pole with a metal hook on the end and retrieved it that day.

A little later, at the end of the garden, I saw pale figures climbing the wall into our garden. Then I recognized them as escaping prisoners to whom I had spoken on my visits to the prison when I had been locked into the cage while talking to them. They told us they were off now. A well dressed man came in and wanted to stay. He had a walking stick, a thing the Chinese never used. This made me suspicious and we sent him away. I think he must have had important papers in the stick!

As it got dark we had a visit from a school master whom I had baptised when he was a student. He had a leather belt and a revolver in it. He asked us not to sleep upstairs as there might be shooting, and not to open the main gate to anyone, whoever they might be. Jessie writes:

'That night, having settled ourselves downstairs, we read Psalm 91 together, and took comfort. While the local militia were in control, we were allowed a certain amount of freedom, but as soon as the Northern Army reached us things were very different. Suspicion was rife and friend betrayed friend; relations betrayed their own folk. There was no justice, no trials, and people just disappeared in the night without any reason. During this time I carried on with the dispensary and midwifery, very conscious of God's keeping power, for any mishap might mean prison. We had a quiet Christmas and services went on as usual. One night we had some of the Northern army quartered on us with their womenfolk. The field telephone was going all night and it was impossible to sleep. We had an army doctor quartered on us for six weeks who at first would not deign to see us. However, the children soon broke down his reserve and in the end, on leaving he accepted a Gospel offered to him. Sharing our kitchen with his orderly was not a happy arrangement, as he always wasted hot water when we had got some ready for our meal.

'Sometimes we would see soldiers coming in to look for utensils to "borrow" and we had an arrangement that as soon as we saw them, the cook handed the pots and pans in at the back window and I locked them in a cupboard. I felt rather like a jailor. Buying and housekeeping were difficult, because one had to know just the right time to sell our bales of cotton yarn for rice. We lived a rather hand to mouth existence, but as someone has said, "the hand was the hand of God" and that made all the difference. Just at the right time a patient would pay for medicines with eggs or rice or some other commodity, or someone would have a feast and kill a pig and bring us a piece of pork or some fruit. It was wonderful to be so dependent on God and to see His hand providing for our need.'

About this time a Communist general sent for Jessie. His wife had a 'blue' baby. Jessie saw that nothing could be done; so did not prescribe. The next day the baby died. Had she prescribed, there might have been deep trouble.

Another time I saw two soldiers coming up the garden path as we had our lunch. At that time in the Communist army, men and officers wore the same uniform. I went down the path to meet them, but they insisted on coming in and sitting down. Presently one of them said "Can you tell me where I can get a glass eye?" I told him that Canton would be the nearest place. They stayed a little longer and then left. I escorted them to the street. There I saw a bodyguard of soldiers waiting for them. Later, when I was in Nanning, I saw postcards of the four leading Communist generals. One of them was Liu Po Chen, the one-eyed general! It was he who had come in and asked. Later I saw him riding on a magnificent horse in the town.

In the January, I went down with hepatitis, and was quite ill. When I was feeling a little better, Jill who was then 15 months old, became ill. We were not sure at the time what was the matter with her but she was clearly in some pain. Later we thought it was possible she had contracted hepatitis also. We were not able to travel, and we could not contact the Hospital, and in the afternoon, after only six hours of illness, the Lord took Jill quickly and quietly as she lay in Jessie's arms. I carried the little coffin out to the road and to the little Christian burial ground where she was laid to rest. We had a gravestone made in the shape of a cross on which were the words from St John's gospel: "Verily, verily, I say unto you, The hour is coming, and now is, when the dead shall hear the voice of the Son of God: and they that hear shall live." Her English and her Chinese names were written on the gravestone. We felt the stone would be a witness, after we had left.

The Pesketts and Iris Critchell, missionaries from the Hospital, came out from Nanning for the funeral and took us back to the capital with them.

Jessie continues: 'Our return later was very hard, for the gap left was tremendous, but God had work for us to do and He gave us His promise, "My grace is sufficient for thee," so we proved it true. Christopher then had convulsions and we wondered for a time if God was going to ask us for another of our little sons. However, he recovered and the work went on. There were still needy folk to tend, refugees to help ... Outpatients were as numerous as usual and midwifery cases booking up. I was sometimes called up in the middle of the night and once had an escort of Communist soldiers to a woman in need, because there was a curfew and we were not allowed on the streets at night.'

About this time, I had one or two visits from a Communist army officer, a doctor. He told me he was a Christian and his family and we had talks together. If I remember rightly, we prayed together. He invited me to visit him in Sheung K'iu, a market town about seven miles away. He told us where to find him. We cycled over and found him. He then took us into a long one-storey building which had a wall across the centre. He invited us to sit down, then went carefully round to see if there was anybody in the other side of the building who could hear us. He then explained that he and his wife had kept their son with them, but it was likely that he would be sent elsewhere. Would I be willing to baptize him as he had never been baptized? They hoped he would be baptized before he left them. I hesitated. We had a little congregation in that market town and I wondered how I could arrange it. In the end I said I would get in touch with him again.

In fact, I never saw him again. Had I realized, I would have baptized him then and there. I was deeply sorry. He was from Manchuria. How difficult it was to make decisions under these circumstances.

We found it increasingly difficult to carry on and began to realize that our presence was making things difficult for the Chinese Christians. They were being accused of being "the running dogs of the Imperialists". By this time I had completed the translation of St Mark's Gospel into the Zhuang language, using a North China phonetic script. It was written in a large, thick exercise book. The translation had taken at least six months to do with the help of my Zhuang teacher. Though I could speak in Zhuang I was never fluent enough to preach in it.

Jessie was still busy with her nursing and midwifery. One day an urgent message came asking us to visit a case some seven miles away. We cycled over and before we reached the house, could hear piercing screams. The woman expecting the baby was unable to urinate, and was in agony. The difficulty was that according to local custom, she must not see light while the pregnancy continued. At last they covered her over with blankets and produced a little peanut oil lamp, and Jessie was able to insert a catheter and the screams quickly subsided. Later she had a successful birth. On another occasion she treated an old blind woman. She had been a concubine, had been unfaithful and her husband had stuck needles into both eyes. She was ingrained with dirt, having never washed. Jessie insisted on bathing her in a Chinese bath, much against her will and got her cleaned up.

Once I was visiting Nanning on the bus and had a small suitcase with me. On arrival the Secret Police asked me to open the case. They took everything out and looked under the piece of paper at the bottom. Under it was a Chinese visiting card, the card of an old general, who a long time earlier had asked me for an introduction to a Hospital in Liuchow. The security man said:

"Is this a Communist General?"

"No."

"Is he a Nationalist General?"

I said "Yes."

"What are you to do with him?" he asked.

I saw I was going to be in real trouble. "Well," I said, "He was an old man and was sick and he asked me to give him an introduction to the Hospital." He obviously did not believe a word I had said and I saw that things were not going well, but there was a little crowd of local people who had been listening, and they all nodded their heads and said "Yes, that was quite true; he was ill and went to Liuchow." So I was saved from a very awkward situation. How good the Lord was to arrange that these folk were there.

At last, in 1950, we applied for permission to leave. As the news of our imminent departure spread, we had an invitation to a Chinese feast from the Headmaster of the Middle School and Mrs Hoh, who with their family were Christians. Their house was only a stone's throw from the Secret Police Headquarters, and the feast was at night outside and fully lit up. It was a very brave thing to do when any known contact with us would certainly create suspicion and possibly even the danger of arrest.

Jessie had no desire to leave, except for the sake of the children, the two who were in England, the two in Hong Kong. She was very happy treating her women patients and her midwifery cases, but she realized too that we were now making it difficult for the Chinese Christians and agreed with me that it was the best thing for us to do.

What were we to do with the manuscript of St Mark's Gospel? Written in a large exercise book it would create suspicion outside the area where the language was spoken. So I decided to take it to the Secret Police and ask them to examine it and certify what it was. I saw the head man and asked him would he put his stamp on it. He refused and said, "The best thing you can do is to burn it."

"But," I said, "it has taken months of work to produce it."

"You burn it," he said.

So then we had to decide whether to leave it behind or to smuggle it out. We decided to take it with us and to put it in the luggage, but place it on top of a case, for we were sure they would search down below.

After waiting for weeks, one day I happened to see the Chief of Police as we walked and he said, "Would you like to go? The permits have come." So we prepared. We had to give a list of any instruments we were taking with us. On my list was "Record Player". When I took the list to the Chief of Police, he was just going to strike his pen through this as he said "Oh, you will let me have that." I objected and said they were very expensive. He replied, "You can buy another," but did not strike his pen through it.

On the day we were to leave, our lorry from Nanning came and they decided to search the luggage before loading on to the lorry. They passed things quite quickly, but when they came to the Record Player, the man searching said, "You are going to give that to the Chief of Police."

"No," I said. Then they became difficult and asked to have back the boxes of records, already loaded on the lorry. As I went to get them the text came to me "Give to him that asketh." I could see that we would never get away as it was. So I sent a message to the Chief of Police, "Please will you look after the Record Player for me till we come back again." This was in order to save his face! Then they were all smiles. Ten minutes later there was a message from the Chief of Police, "Take your Record Player, I don't want it." I think he was afraid he might get reported when we went through Nanning.

So sadly and reluctantly we said goodbye to Wu Ming and got into the lorry. We left the Church in the hands of the Chinese minister, Philip Wong, but Jessie's work could not be continued.

We stopped at Sheung K'iu; here the old lady who had been running the services was standing at the roadside with tears pouring down her cheeks as she said "goodbye". She had kept the little congregation together translating the Bible passages each Sunday into the Zhuang language and explaining them. It was with very real sorrow that we left these Christian brothers and sisters. Later I got a verse from Isaiah 40, v 11 which encouraged us in thinking of them, 'He shall feed his flock like a Shepherd; he shall gather the lambs in his arms,' and we were, many years later, to find how true the promise was.

At Nanning we got passages on one of the river boats. As I stepped on to the 'bluebottle', I saw a Chinese business man who owned the cinema in Nanning. As I passed, he refused to recognise me, but a while later I found myself standing with him on the bows of the vessel, with no one else near, I asked him if he was going to Canton. He replied in a whisper, "No, to Hong Kong." I gave him my address in Hong Kong. After we had been in Hong Kong a few days, I heard a knock at the door, and there was the business man, clothed in beautiful silks. "I had to leave everything," he said. "Conditions were becoming so bad. Several of us were committing suicide." This was his reaction to the new conditions.

Meanwhile, back in the 'bluebottle', the hold was filled with bales of duck feathers. The next day as we were progressing down the river, we heard the sound of a shot and then realized that we were under fire from the river bank. We quickly got the children down into the hold between banks of duck feathers, a splendid screen from bullets. Christopher had left his favourite 'Dodo', a teddy bear, in the cabin, so I had to go back and rescue it!

At last we arrived in Canton; Jessie and the two children stayed on the boat while I was taken to the Police Station to be interrogated. It was nearly an hour before I got back and poor Jessie was worried as to what had happened to me, fearing the worst. When reunited, we proceeded to the railway station to catch a train for Hong Kong. On the journey down the river our luggage had been searched nine times, but each time the exercise book had escaped notice. Now in Canton we were told that there would be a very close search.

The only through train to Hong Kong left at 11.00 am. We got our luggage on to the station only to find, after they had weighed it, that this had taken so long that the train had already left and so our luggage was left unsearched. Stranded in Canton, what were we to do? Jessie wrote:

'We had to choose whether we should go on the afternoon train and spend the night at the border or wait till the next day. We sat there on the platform and prayed for God's guidance and it turned out that what seemed a great disappointment for us was His appointment. We arrived in the dark at the border and followed an unknown guide to a shack which went by the misnomer of an "inn". Here we tried to sleep in our clothes. At 6 am we started out for the station, and found our luggage.'

We needed porters to carry the luggage over the bridge into Hong Kong territory. I bargained with them. They wanted a fabulous price. I asked why so much. They replied that there would be a meticulous search by the Secret Police which might take four hours and they would have to wait. At last I agreed, and we set out. We passed the Customs building and went on. The first thing I saw was an English Police Officer - "Welcome to Hong Kong," he said.

What had happened was that as there had been no train from Canton, the Secret Police were on the other side searching those going into China. So by missing the train, we had missed the search and our precious translation was safely out of China. How thankful we were as we leant back in the train on its way to Kowloon station. All the strain over - safe with our children and very soon united with Rachel and Rosemary. Jessie wrote:

'God had opened the door and shut their eyes. How marvellous is His loving kindness. We were soon in the train and got a drink for the children and changed our crumpled dress for arriving in Hong Kong. I shall never forget the feeling of relief as I stood on Kowloon platform with tears pouring down my face as we thanked God for bringing us safely through.'

12

Back in England

It was not long before we got a passage home to England. On the voyage we had one fright. Joan was on deck with us. The lunch bell went and there was no sign of her. She was just old enough to climb the rails at the ship's side. We hunted everywhere without success, the lounges, cabins, etc. but there was no sign of her. Where could she have gone? At last we found her in the First Class barber's shop, sitting on the floor watching what was going on. How thankful we were to find her safe.

On arrival in England, we had to think out what would be the next step. I still hoped to be able to go on with the tribal language and even continue translation. For this a country parish would offer the best opportunity. We also wanted to have the whole family together after being separated for two years from Rachel and Rosemary, and four years from Margaret and Audrey. In 1951 an invitation from the Chaplain in Chief, Royal Air Force, whom I had taught in Bristol, seemed ideal.

The parish of Dowdeswell, near Cheltenham, was a small country parish. There were good schools in Cheltenham, four miles away. The family could be together as they would be day girls. In the parish was the R.A.F. Chaplain's school. So after prayer we accepted the living, only to be faced with the problem of the previous rector wanting to withdraw his resignation. We did not feel that this was really right, so felt we must decline. Eventually, however, we accepted and moved into the eight-bedroomed Cotswold vicarage on a hillside overlooking a valley and reservoir.

The vicarage was fairly primitive: in the early days the children had to do their homework by candlelight in a large airing cupboard to keep warm as there was no heating. There was also a huge garden including three paddocks to deal with. However, Jessie loved gardening and was to spend a great deal of time in this one. We later used the paddocks for goats and hens and were loaned two ponies for a while for the children to ride. At our own expense we had electric lighting put in and with an Aga to help, we survived the cold weather. The Lord undertook as He had done throughout our lives.

Schooling was a problem. Margaret had passed the eleven plus. Audrey had not. We had banked on Pate's Grammar School for the three older ones, but, when we took Rachel to see her, the Headmistress told us that she would accept Margaret, but not Audrey. She interviewed Rachel for a few minutes. As Rachel came out in tears, the Headmistress told us that she thought Rachel was not fit for a secondary school education! So that door had definitely closed. We felt we wanted all of them to be together, as they had been separated for so long. So we prayed very definitely that the Lord would provide. There was a private girls' school, but we were not impressed with it. The only other was the Cheltenham Ladies College. We had never dreamt of sending them there. It was very difficult to get places and the fees were prohibitive. It was only with the greatest trepidation that I asked for an interview with the Principal, Miss Popham. I explained our situation, having just returned from China. After talking for some time she said, "I will accept all three as day girls without any exams, but I cannot reduce the fees. Let me know what you decide."

I went out and sat on a seat in the Promenade, quite overcome. What could we do? We had a small capital sum but it would not last more than two or three years, and there were the other three to think of. It seemed an impossible opening and yet it was the only door that had opened. We prayed and thought it over. At last we felt that as the Lord had opened this door, we must enter in faith and trust Him to provide as time went on. So I wrote back and accepted the places, preparing to use our capital to pay the fees. She replied, "Bring Rachel on Saturday at nine and call for her at twelve." My heart sank. I was sure Rachel might let us down having had only about two years of formal education, and the whole plan be wrecked. In fear and trembling we left her at nine. At twelve, expecting the worst, we called for her. She came running out, "I like this place."

"Who did you see?"

"I saw the Headmistress and the Headmaster."

"And who is the Headmaster?" I asked.

Rachel replied, "The Headmistress has a little dog and he is the Headmaster." She had been seen by six mistresses. A day or two later I had a message from the Principal: "Rachel is quite up to the standard, but a little weak in English with being abroad." How we praised God. But the uniforms, all second hand, cost a great deal to begin with. And what about the future financially? We had to be very careful with everything we spent. We started to keep goats. I would milk them in the morning, Jessie in the evening. The children helped to tether them out before school. We were able to sell fruit from the garden, which helped, and we kept hens.

In the parish we were able to do house visiting, but central meetings were difficult as there was no church hall and the church and vicarage were nearly a mile from the village. Jessie started a women's meeting and took an active part in the local Women's Institute. It was not long before I was asked to give weekly Bible Studies in the Cheltenham Y.M.C.A. and a weekly morning of lectures in St Michael's House, the women's Theological College in Oxford.

After the first year or two very little news came of the church in China and, I am sure wrongly, my interest in the work I had been doing in China dimmed. The manuscript of St Mark's Gospel got laid aside and also the study of the language. About this time I was invited to become Overseas Secretary for the B.C.M.S., but we did not feel it was the Lord's call, though I did take on editing the Missionary Messenger for some years.

How we were to have holidays with six children seemed a real problem, but the Lord provided. The Caravan Mission to Village Children were selling their old caravan and I bought it for £25. It was a very old caravan with a lantern roof but this served us for several years and enabled us to join the beach mission in Bude, Cornwall, and I was able to take Bible studies each morning for the parents. This continued for a number of years.

Meanwhile our little capital was steadily growing smaller. What could we do? We were sure the Lord had made it possible to send the older three to the Ladies' College. Would he provide? Another year or so and our capital would have gone. We decided to approach the Gloucestershire Education Officer, and I wrote to him. He was sympathetic, but could see no way to help us, but if I would like to see him, he would arrange a time. So I saw him and explained the situation to him. He said he would like to help, but could see no way to do so, but he was going to London in a day or two to see the Minister, and would see if anything could be done. So we prayed.

A day or two later he wrote and said that he had seen the Minister and they had decided to pay the full fees for all three all the time they were at the Ladies' College, and their travelling expenses, and would repay what had already been expended. We were thrilled with gratitude to our Heavenly Father. He had provided, "good measure, pressed down and flowing over." The Education Officer told me that they did this because when in China, with both parents abroad, we could have claimed their fees at Clarendon for the two older ones, and so they would do this instead of repaying back bills. So our hearts overflowed with gratitude.

The Principal had said that if we wanted Rosemary to go to the Ladies' College, she ought to be at New Court School, a preparatory school in Cheltenham. So I wrote to the Headmistress, Miss Peplow, and arranged an interview. Then I saw in the paper that the fees were going up, so I phoned to cancel the appointment. She rang back, "No, don't cancel it. come and see me." So I went and we talked. "Could you manage half fees?" she asked. "Yes, I'm sure we could," I replied. When the time came she did this too for Joan.

I had hoped that Christopher would go to Monkton Combe, but it seemed quite impossible to think of a boarding school; however, my brother, Godfrey, who had been headmaster at the Cathedral School in Lahore, promised to see him through, so the Lord had provided for all the family. How thankful we both were.

Earlier on I can remember kneeling in the church at Dowdeswell and telling the Lord what a wonderful thing it would be if the church were full and so His name glorified. I cannot remember which year it was, but the two headmistresses of Oriel School, who had come sometimes in the holidays approached me and asked if it would be possible for them to bring the boarders to Dowdeswell Church in term time. They would hire a double decker bus. I said that we could certainly arrange it and would be delighted. Among the girls who came were three nieces of the President of Liberia. So our morning services became very well attended in term time - a church full of schoolgirls, besides the ordinary congregation. Three African girls from the school made their homes with us in the holidays for one or two years.

Meanwhile the Red Guard movement had begun in China and there was no possibility of contacting the church there; church buildings were all closed and taken over, Bibles and Christian literature burnt.

This caused us to feel, perhaps faithlessly, that our part there had ended. The Bishop of Hong Kong, R.O. Hall, in the last letter he sent me, said, "I think we can take it for granted that you and I will never see China again." But we did go on praying for China.

As they were growing up, the family began to disperse and, in 1963, the desire began to come into my mind to do some Biblical research. I had been lecturing at St Michael's House on the Epistle to the Hebrews. So I began to pray about this. I was determined not to make the mistake I had made earlier with Chinese research, but as I thought and prayed, the Lord seemed to bless the idea. So I approached three of the Oxford Colleges. One did not answer; a second suggested approaching St Catherine's. The third, Lincoln, sent me a telegram arranging an interview and offered a place if the Board of Theology accepted the field of research. Finally, it was decided that the thesis should be 'The Jewish background to the Epistle to the Hebrews, with special reference to the Dead Sea Scrolls.' My supervisor was to be the Reverend C. S. C. Williams of Merton and we talked it over together.

The question then became how was I to give the parish the care it needed and keep term in Oxford - four nights a week in term time? and how could I afford to travel there and back? And where was I to sleep in Oxford? But the Lord undertook in all these problems. St Michael's House let me park the caravan there. This plan was alright until early November, when I woke to find icicles hanging from the ceiling in the caravan, and the whole ceiling a sheet of ice! I knew the Professor of Chinese, Professor Dubs, and a day or two later was jokingly telling him about the episode. A little later, Mrs Dubs contacted me and said, "We have a spare bedroom which needs airing. Would you be so good as to come and sleep in it?" So for the rest of my time at Oxford I had the luxury of a bedroom with an electric blanket in cold weather. How generously the Lord had provided.

I decided on a plan which would give me four nights in Oxford and five days in the parish and I decided to hitch-hike, wearing a clerical collar. I had no difficulty with lifts and was never left stranded.

About a month later I saw my supervisor and told him that I felt that ,after twenty years without studying, I should never catch up and I had better give the idea up. However, he was most encouraging and urged me to continue. He carefully supervised me, and under Professor Driver, we went right through the Dead Sea Scrolls, a great privilege.

At last I got the Thesis completed and faced the oral. One of the examiners was the one whom my supervisor had said he hoped I would not get. So I entered for the B Litt and presented my thesis. To present the thesis I needed my supervisor's signature, so I went to his home in Holy Well and knocked. I asked if he was in. His wife said that he was not. I asked if I could see him at the College. She then let me know that that morning he had died of a heart attack. I was terribly shocked but I was so glad that a little later I was able to attend his Memorial Service in Merton chapel. I had a warm affection for him. When the results came, I found the thesis had been accepted.

The degree ceremony in 1963 was in the University Church as the Sheldonian Theatre was being decorated. There was only one other B Litt candidate, a young lady, and as we walked up the central aisle with the deans of our colleges, I could not help thinking how like a wedding it must have looked!

Meanwhile, on the nights when I was in Oxford, Jessie decided that she would offer to the Old People's Hospital in Cheltenham for night duty. She cycled the four miles there and back on each occasion. The ride in was all downhill, but the ride back was uphill, a real test in all weathers. After a bit she got invited by a Women's Institute member to have breakfast each morning with them in Cheltenham. So the Lord had provided for both of us.

Some time before I had been asked to speak at the Gloucester Diocesan Conference on the subject of the Christian Sunday. This had whetted my appetite to go into the subject more fully and after prayer, I decided to apply to do a DPhil thesis on the theological background to the Christian Sunday. There was some hesitation on the part of the Board of Theology as a learned German work had just appeared, *Der Sonntag* by Professor Willy Rordorf. However, as I told my new supervisor, Dr S.L. Greenslade, it was especially the Theological side that I wanted to go into and it was accepted. I no longer needed to 'keep term', four nights in Oxford. It required going into the writings of the early Fathers, both Greek and Latin, and this I found most interesting.

During our last year or so at Dowdeswell, we had three weddings, Migi, Audrey and Rachel. We decided to clean up the old Tithe Barn in the garden and it made a lovely setting for the receptions after the services in Dowdeswell Church.

About this time I was approached with an invitation to go to Cambridge to be Vicar of St Philip's Church. So Jessie and I drove over to see the church and vicarage, and to talk to the churchwardens. The church was not attractive outside, but quite nice inside. The last two vicars had been there each for thirty-three years. The churchwardens showed us over the vicarage. It was all dark wallpaper and dark paint. One of them remarked, "Sir, I'm afraid this will put you off!" But we had been in much worse dwellings in China. After much thought and prayer we accepted the offer and got ready to move.

Then the question arose with Oxford University whether we would like to transfer to Cambridge to do the DPhil. I said I would rather remain on the books of Oxford University. Finally, it was solved. Oxford would agree to consider that Cambridge was "in the vicinity of Oxford!" It was now much easier to make use of the University Library in Cambridge than the Bodleian, though I had occasionally to go to see my supervisor in Oxford. When I had completed the thesis and presented it, it was accepted. So we praised the Lord.

Meanwhile, Jessie got busy with the Mother's Union branch there and began to help with the women's side of the work. It was a typical town parish of about 6,000. In the parish of Mill Road was the Romsey House Theological College, an interdenominational college, for men and women. They had been praying very much about the appointment when the last vicar had resigned. I was invited to lecture one morning a week on the Epistle to the Hebrews and Comparative Religions. Jessie and I went to lunch there on that day and a warm friendship sprang up with Miss Morris, the Principal, and her staff.

In the summer vacations we continued to go to the Bude Beach Mission and I was able to continue the Bible Studies for parents each morning. I also had the privilege of taking Bible Readings for the Annual Christian Medical Conference in Bournemouth for two years, and the Scripture Union Conference. I also read a paper on the Christian Sunday at Tynedale Fellowship Study groups and was invited to give a Bible reading at the Ely Diocesan Board of Mission on the missionary outlook in the Old Testament.

Jessie, as at Dowdeswell, was having many opportunities to speak at Women's Meetings, not only to churches in Cambridge, but in the area around. Her talks were evidently greatly appreciated, for besides the Mothers' Union at St Philips, she started a Women's Fellowship at St Philip's and spoke at Christ Church, St Barnabas, St Stephens, St Martyn's, The Round Church, Railway Mission, at two Baptist Churches in Cambridge, at Wesley Church, and outside Cambridge at Waterbeach and as far afield as Royston.

13

The Call to Kenya

It must have been in 1964 that Jessie and I attended the B.C.M.S. Spring Conference in High Leigh. During the Conference the B.C.M.S. Secretary approached me and said that an African student, Paul Lantey, had nowhere to go after the conference. Could we put him up for a few days? We were only too pleased. While he was with us he was talking about his work in Kenya. When he learned that I had taught in a Theological College, he said to me, "Why don't you come and teach in the United Theological College at Limuru in Kenya?" I didn't say anything, but it was a seed thought and I wondered whether perhaps the Lord wanted us there.

St Paul's, the United College, had come into being through Archbishop Beecher, as a development of the Anglican 'St Paul's College'. The three main churches which formed it were the Presbyterian, the Methodist and the Anglican. It had seemed sensible to combine forces in the training for the ministry in the hope that, before long, the churches would draw together and get to know each other. So the teaching job there would mean that we should be influencing the future leaders of all the churches, especially as other churches began to send students to the college.

I was concerned that I had only been at St Philip's for three years. Was it right to leave so soon? The thought persisted and at last I approached my Bishop, Bishop Roberts. He was encouraging and said that for every one who could teach in a Theological College there were ten who could look after a parish. The Parochial Church Council, when I approached them, felt it was the right thing, but what about the family? They did not stand in the way; four of them were married by then.

I wanted to be quite sure of the Lord's leading, so one day I went into the chapel of Ridley Hall, sat there and prayed that we might make no mistakes. The verse came into my mind, 'Except thy presence go with us send us not up hence.' I opened my Bible to look at the passage and saw the words, 'My presence shall go with thee,' and the word 'go' seemed to stand out. So the Lord was sending us and would go with us.

One of our main concerns was what to do with our furniture while we were away. We thought of a cottage, but they were beyond our price range. Then we saw a chapel advertised for sale, price seven hundred and fifty pounds. We decided to go and see it, in Shepreth just outside Cambridge. When we got there, there were people already measuring it. We discovered later that they were Jehovah's Witnesses! The chapel was 50 feet by 25 feet and behind it a schoolroom 25 feet by 12 feet. There was electric light. Christopher, who was with me, thought it would be suitable, so we drove straight back to the agents and asked if it had been sold. "No, but someone has offered £700." I said, "Well, I will pay the £750," and so it became ours. I was able to convert the back building into two rooms where Joan, our unmarried daughter, could sleep and spend her days off. Joan was training at the Westminster Children's Hospital in London at the time. So once again, the Lord had provided for us in a quite unexpected way and made it easier to leave for East Africa.

Kenya had been passing through difficult times before it was granted independence in 1963. The Mau Mau movement had meant that the ordinary way of life had been upset completely. Life in the countryside was very uncertain. With the granting of independence things quietened down, and with Kenyatta adopting a wise policy, things returned more or less to normality.

The College to which we were sent was a United College with an organising body formed from all three churches, which also provided the staff. It was under the guidance of a Presbyterian Principal, Oswald Welsh, when we got there. There were two streams of students, the Diploma Class, and the Certificate Class (not quite up to the Diploma standard). There were some eighty students with wives and families, and there had been some trouble including a student strike a year or two earlier. Students from other churches began to be accepted.

Limuru, where the college was situated, was around30 miles north of Nairobi, at an altitude of 7,000 feet and almost on the Equator. It was in the Kikuyu area; the other main tribal groups were the Luo and the Luya in the West, the Kamba further East, and the Geriama along the coast. The Masai were nomadic; very few had become Christians.

In 1966, when the time came, we were booked on the liner *Kenya Castle*, and driven to the quay at Tilbury. It must have been a big uprooting for Jessie, to set out again for the mission field, and say goodbye to the family, but she was perfectly willing to be led by the Lord. Her duties involved looking after the health of the college staff, students, students' wives and families.

On arrival in Mombasa after a pleasant voyage during which we got to know the wife and children of another member of staff, we found ourselves in difficulties. There had been no application for resident status for Jessie. The immigration official said she could not come ashore! For a few minutes the prospect looked bleak. Then it was decided to issue her a visitor's entry permit for six weeks, while application was made for a resident's permit. So once again difficulties were overcome and we came ashore and took the train for Nairobi.

We caught the single track night train from Mombasa to Nairobi. From sea level, the railway climbs 6,000 feet before reaching Nairobi. It was dark when we left and we retired to our sleeping compartments. As we looked out in the early morning, we could see the shapes of giraffe or wildebeest in the early morning light. By the time we reached Nairobi, it had become much cooler. On arrival, there was no one to meet us, but this was solved a little later when Gordon Hyslop found us on the platform after we had had a cup of coffee.

When we arrived at the C.M.S. Guest House, we were told that before starting teaching, we were to be taken round to the different dioceses in Kenya to enable us to know the different problems facing each diocese.

How different Kenya was compared to China! We found it fascinating to be driven past giraffe and baboons, flamingoes on Lake Naivasha and the pelicans and lily hoppers on Lake Nakuru. We had a warm welcome in the many centres we visited throughout the country.

On one occasion there was nearly tragedy. We were being driven by the African Archdeacon and approached a level crossing on the railway. There are no gates on the level crossings. Just as we were going to cross, a train came round the bend and our driver was just able to pull up in time. We thanked God.

When the tour had ended we settled into our comfortable bungalow with all modern conveniences - so different from China - and I got down to the teaching. Jessie had a special room for her clinic and a daily time for patients to be seen. She had the assistance of the young wife of another member of staff. She wrote out an account of a day's work as follows:

'Breakfast at 7.15 am. Dispensary 8-9 am. College students, headaches, etc. Appointments to be made for dentists, eyes or transport to Hospital; their wives - many suffering from previous neglect at childbirth and needing hospital help, some expecting babies and told to come to the clinic; some needing advice about baby feeding. Some needing to see a doctor on his monthly visits, many with psychological problems; and also the children, coughs and colds, measles, chicken pox, mumps, wrong feeding, tummy troubles, immunization clinic, cuts (fear of tetanus); preventative medicine. Visits to homes of students, and staff. Next - cooking and housework in our home (interrupted). Lunch - rest, then clinics and evening visits. Staff prayer meetings, committees. Supper, reading or sewing by the fire or invite students for a cup of tea or chat. Possibly night calls or someone worried about a child or sudden illness.'

Once again the Lord provided in a special way. We had no car, almost an essential with the long distances in Kenya. The owner of the Bible Depot in Nairobi asked me one day if we had a car. When

I said no, she said that she would like to provide the money for us to buy a car! So very gratefully we accepted and got in touch with the A.A., who helped us to find a suitable one. We made use of this all the time we were in Kenya. How grateful we were to her and to the Lord for providing it in such a wonderful way. It enabled us to go and speak in many different places and to go on holidays and explore the country.

There was a typically English type of church not far from the College. The person who had it built, an old man of over 90, was still in the choir. I had the opportunity of preaching many times there. Every Sunday, there was a communion service in the College, one week Methodist, another Presbyterian and another Anglican. There was also an East African Liturgy.

At that time students, if married, brought their wives and children. Provision was made to teach the wives. Apart from the wives, the teaching in the College was entirely in English. My wife learnt a little Swahili, but I never tried to learn it. In fact, the students knew three languages, their tribal language, Swahili and English. Once a week there was a Revival Fellowship meeting attended by a large section of the students, which Jessie and I attended regularly.

On arrival, I was asked to be Vice Principal. About eighteen months later, while on holiday at Mombasa, the chairman of the council, Canon Capon, asked to have a talk with me. He told me that Mr Welsh was retiring and the Council would like me to become Principal. It was a big responsibility and something that we needed to pray about. But it seemed the Lord's guidance so I accepted. So, after Mr Welsh's retirement, there was a service of institution for the two of us and for the Revd S.Kibicho as Vice Principal in the College Chapel.

Jessie and I felt that the worship side of College life needed to be emphasised and we determined we would be as regular as possible at both morning and evening chapel and we would try to make ourselves as available as possible to the students.

We had a short furlough in England during a summer vacation. The plane came down to refuel at Benghazi and stayed some hours. Only later did we discover that it was the very day of Colonel Gadafi's coup when King Idris was ousted. The news had not reached Benghazi or we might have been held up.

One of the changes which I felt was needed was the way in which candidates were sent to the College. Up till then, any church or the Bishop of a Diocese could send a candidate. Sometimes they seemed immature or not quite suitable, so I suggested that there should be a Selection Board, something on the lines of the Central Advisory Committee for the Training for the Ministry in England. At first there was some opposition, but in the end it was accepted and proved a valuable safeguard. It was to have representatives of the sponsoring churches on the board.

We had an invitation for me to take the Bible Readings at the Keswick Convention in Tanzania. It was to be at the Msalato Centre outside Dodoma, and we were flown there by the Missionary Aviation Fellowship. It was a happy time and we were able to visit the Theological College at Kong Wa, the Hospital at Mvumi, and the remains of the Ground Nut Scheme, with derelict railway, swimming baths, etc. all overgrown by the bush as it took over. This Scheme had been introduced by a socialist governor after the war to produce peanuts on a commercial basis. Unfortunately it proved to be unsuccessful.

We had been asked to accept two students from the African Brotherhood Church. It had been formed from a political movement amongst the Kamba, and included Roman Catholics and Protestants. It had grown considerably.

The Kamba were good singers. Their choirs sang in parts and we invited them to come and sing to the College. They sang splendidly and at the end made a presentation to us. I was given a live cock and Jessie a live hen. So, holding mine by the legs, I had to make a speech thanking them.

When the time came for them to be ordained, we were invited by their Bishop to attend this ceremony. It was in the open air with a canopy of branches over the leaders and important guests. In the centre was the Bishop, on his right the Archdeacon and on his left, the Canon, all in full Roman robes. In the congregation of some 1,500, there were (I think) 15 choirs. A minister gave a 'hot gospel' address and the ordination followed. It was very reverent. All the congregation knelt on the grass. Afterwards there was an auction, including a cow, then a feast. Unfortunately, the Bishop could not speak English so I could not converse with him. The whole service impressed us both deeply and the singing was magnificent.

I also had the privilege of speaking at the Nairobi Keswick Convention; and of being invited to attend the inauguration of the United Reformed Church. This was held at St Andrew's Church, the Presbyterian Church in Nairobi.

Jessie did a great work among the children of students and their wives in the little clinic opposite our bungalow. She had the supervision of midwifery cases.

One call in particular stands out in my memory. It was a Sudanese wife who did not speak Swahili. The woman did not want to go to the hospital at Kikuyu and we did not allow pregnancies at the College. The only person used to the Sudanese was Mr Anderson and one day the husband came to him and said his wife was not happy. It turned out that she was just about to have the baby. My wife and he got her into the waiting car, where she produced the baby! In African fashion they named it 'Rejoice, Motor Car!'

Jessie had always been fond of painting and while in Africa, she made a collection of Kenyan flowers which she painted. Often when we were driving along she would spot some new flower and call on me to stop while she painted it. In all, she painted some 228 varieties. She got the University in Nairobi to name most of them and added in most cases details of where they were found and at what altitudes.

The Mau Mau trouble had ended before we reached Kenya, but towards the end of our time the 'oathing ceremony' trouble broke out. It was amongst the Kikuyu tribe and its objective was to make sure that in the future only a Kikuyu should be President. Gangs would go out and kidnap men or women and compel them to take the oath, a pagan oath over the blood of a goat. We had a Kikuyu lady member of staff who taught the wives. We were fearful that they might come at night, kidnap her and make her take the oath. Jessie insisted that she and the two little girls must occupy our spare room as soon as it got dark and until the morning. So for a fortnight, as soon as it was dark, she came over to our house and occupied our spare bedroom with her two little girls. I also issued bamboo staves to all the students in case they were approached.

I had been teaching the Diploma Class the Epistle to the Hebrews and St John's Gospel. One day I had a deputation from the class stating that they did not think I was giving them the critical views on the Epistle or on St John's Gospel. I replied that they did not need these for the exam and I felt it would perhaps overload their studies, but I was quite willing and would certainly do this.

In the Autumn term I had a deputation from the Second Year Diploma Class, who would be the third year in the New Year, saying that they would like someone else to take these subjects and not me. I told them that I would think and pray over this request. As I have mentioned, a year or two before I came to the College there had been a students' strike and they had got what they wanted.

As I prayed and thought over it, I felt strongly that it would not be for the good of the College or for the church in Kenya as a whole, to fall in with their wishes. Had I felt I was not capable, I would certainly have agreed with them. So I let them know that, after praying over it, I could not see my way to fall in with their wishes, but I was quite willing, if they did not wish to attend any lectures, to oversee their private reading for the exam.

After the vacation, as the new term started, they came again and repeated their request, and I replied as I had before. I tried to speak to them individually, but the result was they appealed to the other members of staff and asked them to intervene. I had thought that the staff would support me, but they seemed afraid of another strike.

At last an emergency meeting of the College Council was called. This Council consisted of representatives of all three churches. The night before, there had been a meeting of the Revival Fellowship and I had asked for their prayers as a confrontation might involve my resignation. One of the students fell down in a dead faint from shock, and my wife ran over to render help, but he quickly recovered.

At the Council Meeting, I was summoned and explained the situation and that I felt that to agree would be bad for the College, for the students themselves, and for the church in Kenya as a whole. I had prayed very definitely that there might not be in me any spirit of pride or obstinacy, but that I might know God's will, but had still felt the stand I was taking was the right one. Then I was asked to leave and they continued to discuss the matter. At last, after 11 pm, I was informed that they had accepted my resignation (though I had not resigned) and temporarily had appointed Mr Gannaway, a member of staff as acting Principal. This would need to be confirmed at a full meeting of the Council.

It was a big shock for me and for Jessie. She had felt as I did. Some of those who heard about the decision suggested I should challenge the decision, but I felt that "the servant of the Lord must not strive" and that I would accept it quietly. One duty still remained. The Archbishop of Canterbury, Dr Ramsey, who was at a Conference Centre next door, wished to look over the College. So I was to show him and Mrs Ramsey round the College. The Archbishop knew nothing of the situation.

The decision of the Emergency Council meeting had to be ratified by a duly constituted meeting on 25 March. Till then, it was a temporary situation. Meanwhile, I decided to do a tour of some of the areas in the West and North, but I was finding that my appetite was going and I was becoming terribly thirsty. I drove Jessie to Kisumu and then to Kericho, but felt more and more unwell, and decided to call off the visit to Eldoret. On the way back to the College, I had to pass Naivasha, so we called on Dr Bunny and asked his opinion. I had not had any pain and he decided it was malaria and gave me some pills.

That night I felt much worse and felt as if I could not continue any longer. Jessie suggested having a drink of cold milk and this eased things, but as we had no doctor I got one of the staff to drive me to Nairobi in the evening, where I knew I could see Dr Winteler, the heart specialist, as he went into a Graduates' Fellowship meeting. He listened as I told him about the nausea and thirstiness. He wrote a chit and I was, within a short time, in the Nairobi Hospital, where, after the meeting, he came that evening and examined me. Later, after X-rays, I was told that I had stones in both kidneys. One was not functioning at all, and the other only one third, and they would have to operate. The night before the operation was the date for the full Council meeting and I asked if I might be allowed to attend it; however, this was categorically forbidden.

After the operation, Jessie approached a nurse and asked about the result and the nurse replied that she should wait until the surgeon came. This made her think that things had gone wrong. In fact, all was well and the operation was quite successful, but it would take some time to get over. I was not to do anything for three months.

The meeting of the Council on 25 March 1970, decided to uphold the temporary decision, but the voting was, I think, 21 -16. I was encouraged to receive a letter from the Bible Society Secretary, John Mpaai, saying that he thought I had taken the right line, and encouragement too in a talk with Bishop Stephen Neill.

Perhaps I should have given way to the request. It was not a case of black and white, as a number of the students felt I had done right. Though I was cheered when the results of the previous year's exam came through and all had passed in both subjects, this was a sad ending to my service there. I had felt that it was such a vital piece of service affecting the whole church in Kenya. Perhaps, after all, something was done to forward Christ's cause. At least there had been no animosity on my part.

When we left I was able to give a folding aluminium chair to Bishop Obadiah. He had said how much easier it would be as he went round his Diocese to have such a chair.

Jessie and one or two of the staff wives did the packing as I was not allowed to do anything. After a stay of a few weeks in Kiambu and Nairobi, we flew back to England.

14

Back to England and
Visits to China and Kenya

Meanwhile, under the very efficient care of a trained nurse night and day (Jessie), I made good progress and felt stronger day by day. We were praying very definitely to know what the next step should be.

Tentatively, I approached the Bishop of Salisbury and the Bishop of Portsmouth, but neither had anything to offer. On meeting the Bishop of Ely in 1970, whom of course, I had known before, he asked me what I was going to do. I replied that we were waiting for 'the cloud' to lead the way. "I wonder if I could help the cloud," he replied. A few days later I received a message that he would like me to take the Old Age Pension and the Clergy Pension and go and live in the Rectory at Croxton and look after the two parishes of Eltisley and Croxton.

The two parishes of Croxton and Eltisley had been joined together for several hundred years. The parish of Eltisley consisted of about five hundred people; Croxton, which had been much larger, had now some one hundred.

The Newton family had been lords of the manor for one hundred and fifty years, and lived in Croxton Park, and until recently had owned both villages. Lady Myra Fox, who was the daughter of the last member of the Newton family, was the patron of both livings. With the Enclosure Acts, Croxton church had become an island in the estate, the village having been moved so as to make space for a lake in front of the mansion. The Rectory was situated within easy distance of both churches. In Croxton church the Newton family had their family pew, an area enclosed with a screen and containing two sofas, embroidered by Lady Fox's mother. In the churchyard was the family vault. On Sundays, Lady Fox was generally present in church, and if she had a houseparty, it was a full pew.

I was asked if I would go and see the Patron, Lady Myra Fox, at Croxton Park. We both felt that this might be God's opening for us. So, with the Archdeacon, we went to meet Lady Fox. There had been talk of closing Croxton Church as the attendance was so small. Lady Fox seemed quite pleased to see us and decided that we were the right people to be there. The Archdeacon had warned me that with Lady Fox it was a feudal system. There was no consulting with Church Councils or church wardens, though we did meet the wardens at Eltisley. So, in July 1970, after the three months had elapsed, we settled into Croxton Rectory, which had a large garden and an orchard.

I determined that before trying to meet their spiritual needs, I would visit and get to know all in both parishes. As there was no church hall in either parish, meetings had to be held in the Rectory sitting room.

It had been Lady Fox's custom after the service to go to the church door and thank anyone who was present, but as I liked to shake hands after the service, she was not able to do this. She was very autocratic; she could, I found out, be very difficult, but could also be extremely kind and was concerned with any cases of sickness or trouble in the village.

Jessie delighted in the garden and was soon busy in it. Gradually she began to get a little Bible study group started in Eltisley. As soon as Romsey House in Cambridge found we had come into the Diocese again, I was drawn in for one morning a week's teaching Hebrews and Comparative Religions, and Jessie and I would stay to lunch, Jessie spending the morning doing the week's shopping in Cambridge.

Meanwhile, our prayers for China and especially for the Zhuang peoples continued and we began to see changes taking place. The death of Mao Tze Tung and the elimination of the Gang of Four foreshadowed changes, and gradually we saw that contact with the West was a possibility. We waited and prayed in a spirit of expectation.

About half way through our time at Eltisley, the Church Commissioners decided to build a new vicarage in Eltisley and sell the Croxton

Rectory. So we moved into the new vicarage only to find out that there was trouble over access for a car, and for several months we could not bring our car into the garage.

During these years events happened, I believe, through the Lord's goodness, which enabled us to have a good bank balance. The chapel which had met our needs during our stay in Kenya, and our daughter Audrey's needs while she was in Malaya, could now be disposed of. Sewage had been introduced into the village, so its site had become more valuable. While at St Philip's, when I saw two cottages advertised for £550 and £600, I had, as people said foolishly, bought them, though they had sitting tenants and rents could not be raised. The occupants of one decided to buy theirs, and those in the other moved out. So these brought in quite a substantial sum. Perhaps this was sent to enable us to pay for visits later to Kenya and China, for we had begun to realise that with a more liberal attitude embarked on by Teng Hsiao Ping, it might be possible to contact our Christians at Nanning in South China.

My experiences of Beach Missions earlier and the report of Holiday Clubs being held inland turned our thoughts to the possibility of holding a week's Holiday Club in Eltisley during the summer holidays. With the cooperation of the vicar in the next parishes, we held these for several years, led by volunteers from various places. We would have perhaps forty or fifty children attending with Scripture Union activities in the morning and games in the afternoon.

Jessie was able to start a little Women's Fellowship, and I a Bible Study group.

By 1980 we found out that it was possible to make tours into China, one of which was to the three cities of South China - Canton, Kweilin and Nanning. We longed to hear news of how the Christians had fared during the thirty years since we had left. So we decided that we would spend March in Hong Kong and during that time go on the tour of the three cities.

We flew to Hong Kong and stayed with the Bishop Gilbert Baker, whom I had known previously. An army officer met us and took us to the Bishop's house. The next day we went to the China Travel Service to book on the tour. A girl served us and we said that we would like to book on the tour to the three cities. She said, "I am sorry, it is already fully booked for the whole of March."

We had prayed so much about it that this seemed a very sad sequel - to have come all the way to Hong Kong and then not to be able to get to Nanning. However, as we thought and prayed together, we decided that if we could not get to Nanning, at least we would go into China. So the next day we went back to China Travel. The same girl served us and asked where we wanted to go. I replied, "To the Three Cities of South China". "Would you like to go on March 11 or March 18?" she replied, "Though I'm afraid you can't get to Nanning because of the Vietnam war."

"The 18th," I replied, "as the war might be ended by then." So after all we were to go on the Tour. We could hardly believe it and never found out what the reason for the change was.

On the 18th we joined the party and flew to Canton. We were taken to a hotel with 2,000 rooms, and later to see a children's day centre and to the zoo. The next day we were to fly to Kweilin and soon saw the familiar stone mountains we had been so used to in our part of China.

Here we were free to walk about, to talk to students and visit shops. Most were closed and there were no street stalls. We were given a Chinese feast, the first course being flying fox! We noticed that men and women all wore dark blue or dark green clothing.

We were told that the next day's train journey would be to Liuchow, halfway to Nanning, and we would have three days there. There did not seem any possibility of getting to Nanning, but we continued to pray. When we got on the train we found a Cook's party on the train. When I asked them where they were going, they replied "Nanning."

"But," I said, "You can't get there."

"Well, that's our destination." So at Liuchow our party got out and they stayed on. They said I looked very miserable standing on the platform. We were taken to a newly opened hotel and that night to an opera about the Zhuang people, oppressed by Chinese overlords.

During the afternoon we climbed one of the stone mountains and the thought occurred to me, that perhaps Jessie and I might be allowed to go to Nanning as we could speak the language. So I approached the chief guide and said to him, "My wife and I can speak Chinese, couldn't we go to Nanning by ourselves?"

"I will consult," he replied. A little later he said, "Yes, you can go on the morning train and come back in the evening." But that was not what I wanted. "Couldn't we spend the three days in the Friendship Hotel at Nanning?" I asked a little later.

"I will consult," he replied.

"Yes, but you will have to pay extra," he replied. That was no problem, so next morning we caught the train. On arriving in Nanning we were met by a guide and a taxi and taken to the Friendship Hotel. There were army officers everywhere. The population had increased from 90,000 to one and a half million. We went to the Church which I had built. It was still the headquarters of the local Communist Party. We were taken to the newly built bridge across the West River and taken to the Tribal Museum.

We asked the guide whether he would be able to take us to Wu Ming where we had spent our last five years in China, and he agreed. It was no longer a rough road, but metalled. On arriving at Wu Ming we were taken to the local Government offices, which backed on to where we had lived. A young fellow came in, perhaps about 40. When he found I could speak Cantonese he was very thrilled and we chatted together. I thought he was just a clerk. In fact he was the chief man in the county.

After drinking tea, he asked where we would like to go. I said we would like to find the grave of our little girl. It had a stone cross as a gravestone. He took the trouble to walk with us over three grave-yards, but finally decided that the site must have been built over.

We were then to go to the place where we had lived. It was market day and there were crowds of people, most of whom were Zhuang. On arriving at the door of a house, the official knocked and we were invited in. There was quite a crowd of people, many of whom recognized us immediately and brought out chairs and tea. A young fellow dashed across to shake hands. I think he was the son of the woman who as a girl had looked after our children. I could see that the official was very impressed with the reception they had given us. I noticed an old man sitting by the door, so as we went out following the official, I gave him a Gospel in Chinese. We were taken to Ling Shui, the place where a river came out of the rocks, and here was another old man who remembered me playing the concertina when we went out preaching. He too received a Gospel.

Then we were taken back to the Government building for lunch. As we entered the gate a woman was standing there. When she saw Jessie she threw her arms around her. It was Oi Kuang, who had looked after our children when she was fifteen. She was overjoyed to see Jessie. Jessie managed to ask her when they were alone whether they were able to come together for worship, but she said it was not possible.

We were made to pose for photographs, one of the officials holding my hand. So, with the woman, we went in for lunch (Chinese). After a little we heard people coming into the other side of the large room separated from us by a screen. It was the Cook's party off the train. I waited until they had sat down and then peeped round the screen. "How in the world did you get here?" they asked. They were filled with surprise. After lunch the official took us to a beauty spot and then we said "goodbye".

On the journey back to Nanning the local guide asked me to explain the Christian faith to him. So for half an hour, there in Communist China, I explained the gospel to him. He seemed really interested and he too received a Gospel before we parted.

On our return the next day we joined the party at Liuchow and reached Kweilin. The next day we were put on a Russian-built plane for the journey to Canton. When we were well up, the plane began to fill with white smoke. As it turned out this was an idiosyncrasy of the air conditioning! We finally reached Hong Kong safely by train from Canton.

Had we been six months later the Church at Nanning would have already been handed back, as happened in 1981. I have a photograph of some sixty or more of the Christians gathered for a celebration there at that time.

So now we had made contact with China again and Bishop Hall's prophecy had proved wrong.

It was not long before I had got out the translation of St Mark's Gospel, laid aside in my desk for thirty years, and got down to rewriting it in a Romanized script.

About this time Sir Joseph Needham, then the Master of Caius, let me know that a party of Chinese scholars was coming to Cambridge. Would I like to meet them? I said that I certainly would. So he invited me to tea with them. The thought that had occurred to me was that if I could get permission to go back and live where we had been, for three months, I could get to know the language better and perhaps continue translating. I decided to approach only the top man about this. At last I got a seat by him and made the suggestion. He replied, "You write to me in Peking, and I will let you know."

This I did. It was not possible to get permission to live in China for three months, but he enclosed a book on the Zhuang tribe which proved most useful. Later I discovered that the Kwangsi Government had introduced a Romanized script for the Zhuang. So I got down to mastering that and transliterated the whole gospel into that script.

The idea of a trip to Kenya came into our minds later and I wrote to the African Bishops and told them that I would like to meet the Clergy in each diocese and, if convenient, give Bible Readings to them. Unfortunately, as I found out later, the month clashed with a visit of a team of 'Partners in Mission.' Only three of the dioceses felt that it would be possible.

So on 17 November 1981, we reached Nairobi and were met by Mr Highwood, the churchwarden at All Saints, Limuru, and taken to their lovely home. We visited St Paul's College and the next day met the Vicar of St Paul's Church, an old student. Later we visited Bishop Gitari at Embu. Then we went to Kabare and looked over the College there with the Bensons. On the 28th we visited Nakuru and stayed with Bishop Laaden Kamau. I was given the privilege of preaching in the Cathedral and on to a Confirmation service in a church in the wilds. As I was going into the church I found I had a 'soldier ant' in my trousers. Their bite is very painful. What was I to do? In the end I managed to squash it through my trouser pocket and avoided a nasty bite! Later we met some thirty of the clergy and gave a Bible Reading. The Bishop had been most kind.

The next day we caught the train to Mombasa and were met by Richard Mwambanga, a former St Paul's student. At one stage I became very sick and was taken to the hospital. The Professor of Medicine prescribed and I felt better. Later we saw Bishop Crispus, the African Bishop of Mombasa, and on the morrow gave the talk to the Bible School students and one or two clergy. On arrival back, we visited Naivasha and the Bunnys, a B.C.M.S. doctor in Kenya and family.

We reached Kisumu on 7 December. I gave three Bible Readings to the whole of the Diocesan Synod. We met the Bishop and later Bishop Mundia and Bishop Festo Olang.

My son, Christopher, after his ordination by Archbishop Ramsey in 1969 and a curacy in Croydon, had gone abroad. Having been transferred from Ethiopia, he was now Vicar of Arusha, the large town in the north of Tanzania. It was a strategic centre for evangelism. Services were in English and Swahili. So from Kenya we went on to Tanzania to stay over Christmas with Christopher and his wife, Eva. I had the privilege of preaching at the English service in Arusha, but on Christmas Day had a bad tummy and could only eat a piece of toast! I had the chance to visit some of the bush churches before we said "goodbye" and returned to England.

So while we were in semi-retirement the Lord had opened doors of opportunity once more both in China and in Kenya. Jessie too had been able to contact many old friends. One more opportunity was given to preach: this time in a new continent when we were visiting our eldest daughter, Margaret, in America, and preached in their little Episcopal church in Maryland.

In 1971 I was made Chairman of the Romsey House Theological College Council. As such, it fell to my lot to oversee the appointment of a new Principal when Mrs Haberman resigned. The Council was equally divided when the voting came and it fell to me to give the casting vote. I am sure we were guided by the Lord when we appointed Reverend David Greig as Principal.

In June 1984 I took a Golden Wedding service in Croxton Church for the father of my churchwarden, Colonel Peter Williams. It was a very happy service. That afternoon I was going for my regular walk, though Jessie was not with me. How, I do not know, but crossing the A45, I was knocked down by a motor cycle, and taken to Hinchingbrooke Hospital in Huntingdon.

A policeman came to tell Jessie and she was taken by Dr Hill to the Hospital. I was unconscious for two days with bad concussion. On regaining consciousness I found that I had a hairline fracture of one leg and I was seeing double with very bad concussion. It was a very frightening experience for Jessie as she realized all that had happened.

Slowly I began to recover, but found that when taking a walk, once or twice I lost my balance and fell. But within a month I was thanking God for the accident for I could see how I was learning new lessons and it had been used to help my churchwardens at both churches who, apart from the Communion services, ran the services and preached. So I praised God for letting me have the accident.

In the September it was our Golden Wedding Anniversary and we were to have a celebration at the Military College, Shrivenham, where Rachel's husband was on the staff. Christopher had been invalided home with a tropical disease and was in Hospital in London. Margaret was in the States, so we did not expect to have the whole family at the celebration, but about 10.00 am in walked Margaret and a little later Christopher, who had been allowed out. So the family was complete.

How thrilled we were, and full of gratitude to God for his faithfulness over the years. How many times had we experienced his provision and protection. What a privilege it had been to experience together in reality the fulfilment of His promises and to experience the leading of 'the cloud'. He had never failed us. The ravens had never failed.

The first attempt to preach again was at the funeral of the one who had been churchwarden at Eltisley for 35 years, Mr Henry Rose, and I found I could manage to speak again in public. Gradually I felt that it was time to retire. We had bought a house at Heacham in Norfolk to be near Mr and Mrs Haberman, but after the accident, the family felt we ought to be near one of them. Christopher had been installed as Vicar of Harwell, Oxfordshire, so we decided to buy a house there, which we did in 1984.

In 1987 I received a long letter in Chinese asking me to come and visit the church in Nanning. It was from the Reverend Wu Ying Ts'ai, whom I had baptized as a boy in 1937. He had recently been ordained and was Chairman of all the Three Self Churches in Kwangsi. 'Would I come and join in with the developments?' They had built a five-storey edifice some two hundred yards from the church. They would like me to stay there.

Before that, I woke one morning with what felt like acute heart-burn. It was so bad that I rang Chris and he came over and called the doctor. He decided that I had had a coronary and must rest and go quietly. Two other doctors who were consulted agreed with the diagnosis. But my daughter, Audrey, a trained nurse, felt that I had a slightly jaundiced look. She wrote to my doctor and he took this up and in a day or so they had decided that it was not the heart after all, but gallstones. So I went into the John Radcliffe for X-rays and it turned out that this was indeed the trouble.

I had two days of the new type of operation without major surgery, and the trouble was cleared up. How grateful I was that that early promise, "He shall strengthen thine heart" had not failed and the way was opened for me to resume a normal life and to be ready and able to go to China.

Jessie was no longer in a fit condition to travel with me as the early signs of senile dementia had already appeared. The family undertook to care for her, so I accepted the invitation and booked to fly to Hong Kong. It was now possible to fly direct from Canton to Nanning, one hour's flight instead of the long river journey or the train journey via Kweilin. I planned to stay for ten days in Nanning. It was arranged that in Hong Kong I should stay at the Overseas Missionary Fellowship centre in Kowloon. When we had gone in 1980 we had come down at Bahrain on the Persian Gulf, but after leaving Heathrow we were told we would soon be 70 miles south of Moscow and after crossing the Himalayas we landed at Delhi, and from there to Bangkok and across Vietnam to Hong Kong.

On arrival, I could not see anyone to meet me as had been promised, but at last saw Frances Lambert and we went to O.M.F. House. The next day we went down to the Christian Communications Centre and talked over the itinerary. I was next day to take the train to Canton. It had not been possible to book on the plane to Nanning, but someone would meet the train in Canton and we would go to the aerodrome and see if there were any vacant seats. It sounded very   precarious and uncertain, but there was nothing else I could do.

So I had to trust the Lord that accommodation would be found on the plane. We had trusted before, now we must trust again. The train journey was very pleasant - a full train and no propaganda on the loudspeaker. I was met at the other end and we got to the airfield. My companion asked about possible bookings but was told that there were none yet. We waited an hour - still nothing. Two hours - still nothing; but a few minutes later he came back with the booking. I thanked him and went to board the plane.

It was quite a pleasant journey - only an hour - but on arrival I realized that instead of landing at the old aerodrome, we were quite along distance from Nanning; in fact, 20 miles, and there was no one to meet the plane. What was I to do? There was a bus waiting, but I had no idea where it would finally drop me.

There was a taxi with a lady driver. I decided to take that and tell her to drop me off at the road where the five-storey building was. Nanning had changed so enormously that I did not recognise the layout at all. At last we reached Seven Star Road, and looked out for the five-storey building, but after driving up and down she could not find it. So I decided the only thing was to be taken to the Church.

On arrival there I saw an oldish lady sitting on a stool. She was, in fact, the Vicar's wife, and welcomed me in. I showed the taxi driver round the church and invited her to attend on a Sunday. After I had been sitting down for a quarter of an hour, the Reverend Ying Ts'ai and the Vicar, the Reverend Paul Liang, arrived. They had been waiting at the bus terminal for me. It was such a joy to meet them. Paul Liang was Vicar when we left in 1950. He had been in prison on a false charge for 21 years.

We walked over to the five-storey building. As the scaffolding was still up, we had missed it. When we got in Ying Ts'ai told me that I could not stay in the church building. The Police insisted I must stay at the big hotel about a quarter of a mile away by the river. He said he had arranged with a Miss Wang to act as my guide in case I lost my way. So for the rest of my time she escorted me to and fro. She could not have been kinder to me. I learnt that her parents were both Communist Party workers. She was the only Christian in the family and a graduate at Nanking Theological College. She had been influenced by an American who taught English and had invited her to attend a Christmas service. She had known nothing of Christianity before. She was such a help to me and insisted on doing my washing for me.

While in the hotel, I had a knock at the door and in walked an old Chinese man. He grasped my hand and said, "Oh, pastor, thank you so much for introducing me to Christ and baptizing me. It is so wonderful to be a Christian." He was the driver of the lorry which took my wife over the Burma Road. He was so full of gratitude and was still cycling about in the town.

On the Saturday night, I had a bilious attack and woke up on the Sunday morning feeling that I could not face anything that day. But I asked the Lord for his special grace and help and when Miss Wang came later to escort me to church, I was feeling considerably better. There was a full church, probably some three hundred. I was sitting next to the lorry driver. After the service quite a few wanted to meet me and talk and I was given such a warm welcome. I met several of the delegates from other parts of the Province, including the pastor from Liuchow, a little short man with a lovely smile.

I had hoped to be able to get to Wu Ming, but everyone was so busy with the conference and the Short Term Bible School that I was not able to do so, but was taken on a trip to the limestone caves not far away. Here we must have walked over a mile inside the extensive caves.At one point there was a wide area stretching two or three hundred yards in each direction. Here and there were streams of water which disappeared again.

As we were eating only Chinese food, and the bilious attack had made me a little wary, I felt I should curtail my stay and get back to Hong Kong. But on calculating the cost of the hotel and the possibility of having to stay in Canton and finding that Traveller's Cheques could not be cashed in China, I realized I was going to be in real difficulties. I could pay the hotel bill, but there would be nothing over. So I had to let Ying Ts'ai know. It was possible to change the date of the return air ticket, but what was I to do? Ying Ts'ai after a bit returned and handed me three hundred and thirty Chinese dollars, enough to cover the bill. I insisted that I would pay him back, but he insisted that it was a gift. I was so touched. So the Lord had once more met an urgent need and I was so grateful.

Ying Ts'ai and Paul Liang saw me off at the bus station in Nanning and I was soon at the air field. I was not at all sure which plane I was to take; however, it all went smoothly and I was soon back in Canton. Now it was too late to catch a train or a boat and I had no idea where I could get accommodation; I was completely by myself. I wandered round the aerodrome offices and at last found someone. "Was there a plane to Hong Kong that night?" I asked.

"Yes, at 8.00 pm but it was fully booked." Then they seemed to be sorry for me and said "You go and sit in the reception area and I will get you on to it."

I thanked the man and sat there for some hour and a half. Passengers began to arrive in large numbers and it was drawing near the time to board the plane. I looked round apprehensively to see if the man was anywhere around. I had been praying earnestly that I might be able to get on to the plane. Presently, I saw him coming across. He beckoned me to come and buy my ticket. How grateful I was that once more the Lord had provided in my great need and made it possible to get to Hong Kong that night and so get to the O.M.F. House. I went on from there to stay the last few days with the Lamberts in the New Territories, and saw the extensive building projects that had gone on.

I was very glad that I had made the trip and been able to see the surprising changes that had taken place in seven years. When we were there in 1980 half the shops were shut. There were no stalls at the road side. Everyone was dressed in dark blue or dark green, and people's faces looked old and drawn. This time all the shops were open and all kinds of new things could be bought. Next door to the five storey building was a shop that sold motor bicycles and washing machines. Nearly all the younger women were in bright clothes, and there were smiles on people's faces. So it was quite an eye-opener.

What was far more important from my point of view was the development in the Church. In 1980 the building was still the Headquarters of the local Communist Party. Christians did not seem to be gathering for worship in public. Now in the Delegates' Conference there were representatives from perhaps thirty churches in different parts of the Province and with various backgrounds; the Christian and Missionary Alliance, Southern Baptist, Pentecostal, Anglican and Seventh Day Adventists. But what impressed me was the happy way in which they seemed to be working and worshipping together. Far from being on the defensive, the outlook was definitely to plan for the future, and expansion. There seemed to be a spirit of hopefulness and expectation. What did worry me was that in the service on the Sunday there were no children, so different from before liberation. No one under eighteen is allowed to attend services or be baptized.

A source of encouragement, however, was the number of students in the Short Term Bible School who were Zhuang. perhaps over half. This means that they will go back to their home areas and the folk will hear the gospel in their own language. The translation of St Mark's Gospel in Zhuong which I had made years earlier, I recorded on tapes and left with the Minister at Nanning, on this trip. How wonderfully God was answering our prayers that these people might hear the Gospel in their own language and particularly the women, few of whom would know Chinese.

Though I was not permitted by law to preach, I was able to talk to the church leaders and I felt that in spite of the long separation, there was still the spirit of Christian love and fellowship.

Later, I heard from the Reverend Wu Ying Ts'ai that he hoped to rebuild the church in his own village. The original one was built by the Christians of the village themselves. It had been destroyed by the Japanese. I had had the pleasure of being at its opening in 1937. So for the rebuilding I was able to repay him the money which he had so generously given me to pay for the hotel bill.

But meanwhile Jessie's condition was steadily deteriorating and it was my privilege night and day to look after her. More than once she had slipped out of the house without my knowing, in spite of a very careful locking of all doors. Once she had crossed the main road and walked down almost to the Vicarage and been found, completely confused and lost, by a parishioner.

People had told me that I should not be able to stand the constant strain day and night, but early on the Lord had given me the verse in Isaiah 43 V 2 - 'When thou passest through the waters they shall not overflow thee' and I was to find great strength from that. The testing threw me more and more on God's grace and during that time I learnt lessons which I am sure I could not have learnt in any other way. God was teaching me through Jessie's suffering. At times she was her old self and full of affection and love. At times she was uncooperative. Sometimes, but not often, almost aggressive. But what a tremendous privilege it was to be able to repay in some small way all that she had over the years done for me and the family.

In July 1989, the doctor decided she should have a fortnight in the Warneford Hospital in order to give me a break. While there she began to refuse to eat or drink. On my return, a meeting of the hospital staff with the family discussed what should be done. Should they give her electric treatment? While this might be helpful for a time it would not, of course, be a cure. I told them I trusted the Hospital to do what they felt was best. A day or two later she was moved to the little Cottage Hospital in Didcot. Here they gave her the most loving attention and she seemed quite content. I was able to visit her twice a day. Though we constantly tried to get her to take fluids, she remained unwilling to eat or drink.

On 18 August 1989 they reported that her condition had deteriorated and in the evening three of her daughters and I sat round her bed singing hymns. The last hymn we sang was 'The Day Thou gavest, Lord, is Ended' and very quietly and peacefully she stopped breathing. It was all so lovely and quiet. As she went, I said, "Lord now lettest thou thy servant depart in peace," and "Into thy hands we commend her spirit."

Jessie had left instructions about her funeral, 'A service of praise and thanksgiving'. "No prayers for the dead for I shall be satisfied with my Saviour." She had chosen 'When all thy mercies, O my God' and 'When I survey the wondrous cross,' and Psalm 121. The church was full. The service was taken by the Reverend Professor Douglas Spanner and our son-in-law, Philip, gave the talk. I was able to read out the notes of a talk that Jessie had given on 'Friendship with God.' Many said how inspiring the service had been, just as Jessie would have liked.

15

Some Aspects of Jessie's Life

Now that Jessie has gone home, perhaps it may be permitted to trace some of the main lines on which her Christian life was lived.

From 1914, when she was nine years old, until 1933, when she sailed for China, she had kept a spiritual journal. In that journal which has been quoted from in this story, she noted special days and experiences. One day in particular was 11 October, the day when she had publicly committed herself wholly to be Christ's, and to let him choose the path for her. Her birthdays and New Year's Day were also specially remembered. She liked to spend the first few minutes of each New Year's Day in prayer.

Another feature of her Christian life was an assurance that God was leading and planning. When she was faced with difficult decisions she seemed to choose the hard course without ever considering the easier. And, perhaps the most outstanding example of this, was her journey back to Nanning after saying "goodbye" to me in January, 1933, before we were married. It all happened while I was on the liner going to England.

Above Wu Chow, on the West River, she was travelling by herself on a 'bluebottle'. These river boats are about 90 feet long, a large room with bunks at right angles, with entrances only at both ends. There were two little cabins, five feet by five feet, with a women's room at the back over the kitchens. The toilets could only be reached by walking along a duckboard a foot wide on the outside of the vessel, with no rails. These toilets were about two feet by two feet. While the diesel engine was on, the boat shook so much that it was hardly possible to read or write. The one Jessie was travelling on was called *The Bright Star*, and it was towing a large cargo boat. The river was very low. She was by herself in one of the cabins.

The journey lasted for fifteen days, from 1 to 15 February. As I have experienced, one or two days is enough to give one headaches. She might have halved the time had she had anyone with her, as she could have caught a bus about half way, but she felt sure that the Lord had not provided anyone so she was content.

About the third day she wrote about the wearisomeness of the journey and how difficult it was to pray, but consoled herself with the thought that the next time she made the journey, it would be when we were together.

On the fourth day, hardly a third of the way, she wrote, 'This cabin is a holy place where I have been meeting the Lord and learning how to pray. I am so full of joy that we are united in this. There is so much to thank God for.' She speaks of the joy of two lives wholly given over to Him and that our home will be His dwelling place, that she was not grieving over our separation, the pain and emptiness, but having a wonderful peace and joy in God.

She could get little sleep on the fifth day as gambling (mah jong) went on all night. On the sixth day, as they were proceeding, there was a nasty bump as the vessel hit a rock. The passengers got alarmed, but the ship was not holed and she remembered the words, 'The Lord is thy keeper.' How glad she was to lay the whole work at Nanning in God's hands in prayer.

On the eighth day they reached the half way town. She had hoped, if there had been someone with whom she could travel, to catch the bus there and get to Nanning the same day, but she was sure the Lord was overruling.

This was soon followed by the worst part of the river. The water was very low and they had to pass through a series of rapids. So shallow was the water that the passengers walked on the shore for a bit. They were overtaken by another 'bluebottle'.

On the tenth day they spent the whole day getting through the big rapid, 'The Rapid of the Suppressed Wave'. They were walking for several hours. She remarked that they never knew what was going to happen next. But the next day, the second Sunday on board, she praises God that though it seemed tedious, there had been time to pray and think more deeply over things.

On the fourteenth day there was little chance of sleep with Chinese New Year crackers going off at night, but she was stirred by reading 'They shall still bring forth fruit in old age.'

At last, on the 15th, at 2.30 pm they sighted the Hospital at Nanning and she was safely there at last by six o'clock ready for a bath and a meal.

Once she wrote to me, 'Wilfrid, darling, you ask me about the evangelization work. You know, darling, it is the longing of my heart to go out amongst the people. I'd heaps rather be in a difficult place where we were really reaching people, that to settle down always in Nanning and not be able to do so much. And yet, I'm content if that is His will. But, darling, my heart aches for these country women who don't get the opportunity of teaching and I long to be able to speak more so that I could really help them.' She was afraid that if we were in Nanning the Hospital work would prevent us really getting into touch with the country people and especially the women for whom she felt very deeply.

When finally we moved to Wu Ming, and she had the clinic to which the country women came in considerable numbers, she had her heart's desire. The mothers, who so many times had lost their babies on the eighth day through tetanus, were thrilled when she could give them a live baby with no fears. Deeply concerned for the village women in their spiritual needs, she went out with the evangelistic bands before our marriage and made long walks in the heat. On one occasion she caught chickenpox from the villagers and had a very severe attack. When we finally had to leave, the women sent a deputation begging for our return.

She was deeply concerned about the responsibilities of mother-hood, of bringing little ones into the world. She was fond of these lines:

"A partnership with God in motherhood. What purity; what strength; what self control be hers who helps God fashion an immortal soul."

This was her attitude to parenthood. So we left it to God to give us a family as He willed. How she thrilled over each little one as they came, and how terribly she missed the little one God took. Yet there was no grumbling or resentment. On Sunday afternoon, in Dowdeswell particularly, it was a family tradition to sit in the drawing room after tea and each of the children would choose a hymn or chorus to sing. After the last hymn, someone would choose one for Jill, and Jessie's eyes would inevitably fill with tears.

But she believed in this, as in other matters, that the Lord knew best.

About the Lord's day she wrote, 'I love Sundays, don't you? I rather think, Wilfrid, we have the same feeling about His day. To me it is a day specially set aside to worship Him and learn more of fellowship and communion with Him. I think too, don't you? that there are special blessings promised to those who fulfil the conditions and by His Spirit he makes our hearts *delight* in the Lord.'

There are constant references in her letters before we were married on how important she felt prayer was. She writes, 'I long to be more and more used in my prayer life, Wilfrid, don't you? My prayers seem so weak in comparison with all He is prepared to do and how frequently the self-life creeps in.' Then she asks what time I am getting up for my quiet time, and thinks it would be a great help 'if we were both meeting at the Throne of Grace, at any rate part of the time, together.'

* * *

After her death I discovered the notes of the talk she had given, which I read out at her funeral. The talk is headed 'Friendship with God' and describes the friendship characters in the Old Testament and the New had experienced with God. Abraham, for example, was described as a friend of God. Enoch walked with God. God talked with Moses. And in the New Testament, Mary, Martha and Lazarus loved and trusted their Lord. She goes on to analyse what friendship with God means: obedience, purpose, protection, His presence and power, all of which she had experienced throughout her life. The words on her gravestone emphasise the depth of her 'friendship with God':

Lilian Jessie Stott
Went home, 18th August, 1989
"Satisfied with Jesus, my Saviour"